SEED OF FREEDOM

By

AMBER CHYENNE

Hard back : ISBN 979-8-9860716-0-2

Paperback : ISBN 979-8-9860716-1-9

E-Book ISBN:

Published by Amber Chyenne

To my awesome friends, family and, teachers who
encouraged me to write the "Seed 0f Freedom"
And a special thank you to my cover artist "Santhar" for
a fantastic job.
And to my high school teacher MR. D who would not let
me give up on writing the book.

Contents

Dr. Juno's Letter

For anyone who is reading this.

I apologize for the calamity I've brought upon the world. Vice President Linna had told me I was making a cure to stop almost every virus but was using my research to create a weaponized virus. I was foolish to believe her. While I was trying to help the world, she tried to kill off some of the population. They designed it so the symptoms would be similar to the common cold, spread like the flu, and is as lethal as the Marburg virus. As soon as I found out, I destroyed my research, their lab, and their lab rats to prevent it from spreading. In the process of trying to expose Vice President Linna and her plans, she had me arrested and locked away in some remote prison, so I could not be a threat to her plans. If you are reading this letter, do not put your trust in Vice President Linna. She is the devil herself.

JWS

Chapter One

False Hopes

"I love my new lab. The tech is state of the art, and there is so much room. Are you sure it is not too much? Thank you so much vice President Linna." Dr. Juno Willis Smith said, placing a picture of her family on her new desk.

Dr. Juno was the leading scientist in virology. Her hair was light brown with blond highlights, green eyes, and she had a white lab coat on.

"Not a problem. The leading scientist in her field should have the best lab the government has. Now I have an important meeting I must attend. If you need anything, just give me a call." Vice President Linna replied, walking out of the lab and answering the phone, "She is in the lab now. The pieces are in place."

Vice President Linna's hair is solid black in a tight bun. Her eyes were brown, and she wore a suit downed with a matching purse.

It took about an hour for Dr. Juno to finish moving her paper copies of her latest research project from her car to her new lab and filling them away until the following morning. As she finished putting the last file away her cell phone started to ring.

"Hey, honey," Dr. Juno said, while answering her phone.

On the phone with Dr. Juno's husband, Robert Smith, "Just wanted to know if you are staying late tonight."

"No honey, I am just setting the files up and booting the systems up before I leave tonight.," Dr. Juno said, "What do you want for dinner? How does lobster sound?"

It took about an hour for Dr. Juno to drive home from her lab in Philadelphia to their small suburban area. When she pulled into the driveway, her son Oscar was playing basketball with his friends Asher and Simon from down the street. Oscar had short blond hair, blue, and was wearing blue jeans and a solid green shirt on.

Asher has bright red hair, blue eyes and is average height for a 14-year-old.

Simon was a little tall for 14, had black hair, and green eyes.

"Hey, mom. You are looking wonderful. How was your first day at the new lab?" Oscar asked mischievously, walking toward her, "Later guys."

"The new lab was amazing. It is massive and filled with state-of-the-art technology. Is there something you want?" Dr. Juno replied, waiting to see what Oscar wanted.

"What? I don't want anything." Oscar said quickly.

"Okay, then what did you do?" Dr. Juno asked, still waiting for an answer.

"Nothing. What makes you think I did something? Look here comes dad. Okay, I got to go do my homework and talk to you later mom." Oscar dashed inside, knowing he had dug his own hole.

"Hey, honey. How was the drive home?" Robert asked, while hugging her.

Robert is thin 5' 7" man with brown eyes and dirty blond hair.

"The traffic was horrible. How was your day at work?" Dr. Juno replied.

"Good. I have to find a field trip to take my class on. Would it be okay if I brought them to your lab for it? I think they would love it." Robert said.

"I don't see why not. Just make sure the paperwork is completed and give me about a week to have everything set up." Dr. Juno answered.

Oscar departed for the school next morning like he had done every morning, but he did not go to the bus stop. He was sneaking to the skate park since he had been suspended from school. The skate park was run-down and strewn with graffiti.

"Oscar, are you sure this is a good idea? What if we get caught? Your mother will be mad if she finds out." Asher asked, looking around.

"Asher, your dad is a cop, if we get caught, it would be by him, not by my mom. Besides, where are we going to go for the day? We both got suspended for the fight, and if we go to the cafe we will definitely be caught." Oscar pointed out stepping on his skateboard.

"Oscar is right. As long as we stay out of sight, we will be fine." Simon said, going down the half pipe.

"Okay, if you two say so." Asher said right before he stood up grabbing his board.

Right then, Asher's dad passed in a police cruiser. He came to a screeching halt and started to get out.

Officer Jo is 6'2", on the muscular side, red hair, and blue eyes.

"You guys, I think we are busted. There is Asher's dad, and he is coming this way." Simon said, frozen in fear knowing they were caught.

"Hey, dad it's great to see you here." Asher said as he dropped his board.

"Ummu…. I can explain sir. We got suspended because I got into a fight, and they got caught up in it by pulling me off of the other guy. It was my idea for us not to tell anyone." Oscar said quickly.

"Well, even if it is your fault, all three of you boys are to blame because no one said anything. All three of you boys get into the back of my cruiser, and I will take you to the station. After that, I will call your parents and let them know what you have been up to." Asher's father said, pointing at the police cruiser.

Once they had gotten to the station, Asher's dad called Simon's parents first, then Oscar's mother.

"Hello, Dr. Juno Smith. This is Asher's father, Officer Jo. I figured you would like to know that I found our boys at the skatepark." He said.

"Where was he?!! Why on god's green earth was he not at school?!! He is in so much trouble when I get there!!! Thank you so much and I am so sorry for the inconvenience, Officer Jo. I will be there in an hour." Dr. Juno yelled through the phone.

"Ok. I will have him ready when you get here." Officer Jo said, hanging up the phone, "You two have an hour to tell me what started the fight, who threw the first punch, and why in the hell you guys didn't tell us, starting now."

"Well! I threw the first punch, but John started it," Oscar said quickly.

"Ok, if you threw the first punch, then how did John start it?" Officer Jo asked, looking at Asher to answer him.

"He and two of his buddies walked past us at lunch and dumped their milk on our heads. That is when Oscar jumped up and decked him." Asher said, looking at the floor.

"From there, it is kind of explainable. John and I got into a knock-down-drag-out. The only thing Asher and Simon did was pull me off of John while his Buddies grabbed him. I tried to tell the principal, but he would not listen to what I said." Oscar cut in, watching the door, knowing his mom could walk in at any minute.

"Okay, I see why you decked him Oscar, but your mother is not going to like your reasoning behind it because this is the third time this year, with the same kid." Officer Jo said.

"So is Asher in the clear because it was my fault we got suspended" Oscar asked.

"The fight part, yes. Not saying anything negative," Officer Jo said, looking at Asher.

"B.B.B. Officer Jo sir, that was my idea too." Oscar said, reminding Asher's dad.

"That may be true, but it was his choice to go along with it." Officer Jo said.

Right then, the door of the police station slammed shut, and they could hear Dr. Juno heals storming down the hall to Officer Jo's office. When she had reached the door, they could see the anger in her eyes, and her face beat red. It didn't take a rocket scientist to see how much trouble Oscar was in.

"Oscar Baxton Smith!!!!! Suspended again, and this is the third time this year, and it is not even halfway over!! Plus, your teacher just called and informed us that you are failing biology, geometry, and Spanish because you have been suspended three times!!!!! I had to leave early from work to come and get you!!! What if something happened, here we thought you were at school!!! You are failing classes, getting into fights, kicked out of school, and you lied about it!!!!!! I am done with you. You're grounded!!!!!!!!!! There will be no skateboard, skatepark, Xbox, tv, basketball, baseball, or football, as well as no trip to the white house!!!!!!! It will be breakfast, chores, lunch, homework that your teacher gave me for you to do, dinner, shower and bed!!! Until your father and I see fit!" Dr. Juno yelled, "Now go get into the car!!!"

"Dr. Juno, can I speak with you?" Officer Jo asked as she started to walk out the door.

"Yes," she replied, taking a deep breath.

"Oscar was only sticking up for himself, Asher and Simon. There is a student by the name of John that has been giving them hell so far this year. Yes, I think the problem should have been handled better, but Oscar was only trying to protect them." Officer Jo explained to Dr. Juno.

"Okay. Thank you for telling me that." Dr. Juno said.

"He reminds me of his father's brother with that temper. William was always getting into fights." Officer Jo said.

"I know. That is what scares me." Dr. Juno said.

"Don't let it. The difference is that William would get into a fight because someone looked at him wrong. Oscar is getting into fights to stick up for himself and his friends.

His uncle wouldn't have done that. He is a good kid. Cut him a bit of slack. It might help." Officer Jo said.

"Yeah. Maybe you are right. Thank you, Officer Jo." Dr. Juno said, shutting his door.

A week had gone by, and Oscar had been going to work with Dr. Juno.

"Okay, Oscar, your Dad is bringing in his eighth-grade class today. So please make sure you finish your last two papers. That reminds me Vice President Linna will be here afterwards, so you can either stay and meet her, or I can have your father come by on his way home and pick you up." Dr. Juno said.

"I will stay. Thanks, and my papers are already finished." Oscar replied.

In the hall was Robert's class. There are 20 students in his class. They are from the private school that is about 25 miles from Dr. Juno's lab. There are 11 boys in the class. All of them had on red collared shirts with black ties and khaki pants. The nine girls had on a white shirt, black jacket, and black and red pleated skirts that go to their knees.

"Okay, class, meet Dr. Juno Smith. We will be observing her today. Feel free to ask any questions you want because you will be doing a report on what you have learned today. So please pay attention." Robert informed his class as they walked through the sliding glass doors.

"Hello, it is such a pleasure to meet so many bright young minds today. Please feel free to ask any questions. I was told you guys would have to do a report on virology after you leave here that will be due next Monday. So, ask away." Dr. Juno said, waiting for someone to ask a question.

"Dr. Juno, what are you working on right now?" A shorter girl with black hair and brown eyes asked.

"That's a good question. I am working on a super cure. To get rid of almost every illness that can be passed to someone else just by breathing in the same air." Dr. Juno answered.

"Amazing. How long until you have it finished?" A taller boy with chestnut-colored hair and hazel eyes asked.

"It is being tested on lab rats now. I will be moving to human trials in about two months. I want to see more positive results before I move to human testing. I did not catch your names." Dr. Juno replied.

"Oh yes, my name is Rebecca." The shorter girl said.

"And your name is? Young man." Dr. Juno asked, looking at him

"Joseph. Dr. Juno" the boy answered.

The class was there for about two and a half hours before they started to leave.

"Hey, you are the same age as us, right?" Joseph asked. "Yeah. I guess why?" Oscar answered, puzzled.

"Well, your dad is a teacher at our school, and your mom is the leading scientist in her field. You could be going to our school for free, but you are in a public school. I guess I'm trying to ask why." Joseph pointed out.

"Because I have friends there," Oscar explained.

"Joseph, come on, you should be on the bus already," Robert said, walking back in the lab.

"Oh! Sorry, Mr. Smith. Hey, I will talk to you next week, Oscar." Joseph said, racing out the lab doors.

"Are you coming back here next week, dad?" Oscar asked, puzzled.

"No, he is transiting to your school next week. His parents say he needs to make friends. That is when I told them that you went to public school. Maybe you can help him make a few." Robert said, looking at Oscar.

"Sure, I will introduce him to the guys next week." Oscar said, "Bye, dad. By the way, I will be riding home with mom."

"Ok then. Bye guys. Love you two. I got dinner covered." Robert said, walking out to meet the bus.

Vice president Linna and a large muscular man in a black suit arrived an hour after Robert and his students had left. The man was holding a black briefcase and did not say a word before he walked to the other side of the lab just out of Dr. Juno's sight.

"So, how are you doing with your research? Are you ready for human trials?" Vice President Linna asked.

"No, not yet, I want at least eight out of ten rats to be cured and with almost no side effects before moving to human trials." Dr. Juno answered, "Oh, this is my son Oscar."

"Well, nice to meet you, young man." Vice President Linna said. "Nice to meet you too, Vice President Linna," Oscar replied.

While Oscar's mom and Vice President Linna were talking, Oscar started to gather his things. That is when he noticed that the man who came in with Linna was looking through his mother's personal files on her computer .

"What are you doing on my mother's computer? That is in no way public. Who are you?" Oscar questioned the man

"That is none of your concern, young man; go about your day." The man said harshly.

"It is more than my concern! That is my mother's research, and I will not just go about my day! Now get off of my mother's research or get the hell out of her lab now!" Oscar snapped at the man pointing at the door.

"Very well. I am done anyways." the man said as he got up and walked over to Vice President Linna.

Before he walked out, he whispered something in Vice President Linna's ear.

"I am sorry. I must go now. Please Keep me updated and thank you." Vice president Linna said and followed the man out of the lab.

Oscar raced out of the lab after them to confront them.

"I know you two are up to something. There is only one thing on the computer you were on. I will find out why you were on it and what you are doing." Oscar said, looking at both of them.

"Don't be too sure of that young man, even if you do, who will believe some trouble-making kid over the Vice president?" Vice President Linna remarked.

Chapter Two

Deception in the White House

It had been a couple of weeks after Oscar had caught Vice President Linna and the man snooping on his mom's computer. She knew she had to be more careful now that he was on to her.

"Vice President Linna duck!!!" Blake yelled.

Blake is President Carson's 14-year-old son. He had flaming red hair, blue eyes, a slim build, and was of average height.

"Oh. Cassie, please look before you shoot! Thank you, Blake." Vice President Linna yelled, looking at Blake's older sister.

Cassie is President Carson's 16-year-old Daughter. She is 5'4", medium build, has red hair and has green eyes. She stood behind a bright red line on a concrete slab facing a target made for Arrows.

"Look where I am shooting!!!!! You just walked through my Archery range as I let go of the string!!! So, I think you need to pay more attention because I heard Blake try to tell you twice before you walked in front of my target!! I have an idea. Get off that damn phone and look where you are walking!!" Cassie yelled back.

"Mind your manners, young lady." Vice President Linna said as she walked away

"I can't stand her," Cassie said, looking at Blake.

"I hear you there. Something isn't right about her. She sure does spend a lot of time on that phone." Blake said, "Bet I can hack it and figure out why."

"No. Dad said no more hacking after last month. Plus, you are grounded for any tech at all because of it, Blake.

Now come on, there is a tour today with some schools." Cassie said, walking inside.

"Hello. I am President Carson. It is a pleasure to be showing you, students, what I do. Before we start, I would like to introduce my children. This is my daughter Cassie, and this is my son Blake." President Carson said, waving Cassie and Blake to come over to him.

President Carson is 6'2", muscular build, strawberry blonde hair, green eyes, and dressed in a black suit with a purple tie.

"Hi, it's nice to meet some other kids my age." Blake said.

"Hello. Hey dad, I gotta go. I have a lesson with the chief, and she was not happy yesterday because I was late. So, I will meet up with you and this class later." Cassie said, waving bye to her father and Blake.

"Well, I guess it is just Blake joining us for now. Are there any questions?" President Carson remarked.

"I have one. Is the news exaggerating the stuff about the recent terrorist attack on a plane filled with citizens flying to Germany, or should we be worried?" Asher asked.

"Asher. We told you that it was nothing to worry about on the bus. That was closer to Germany, not the United States." Oscar stated.

"For all, we know it could have been a glitch in the navigation system." Simon jumped in.

"I am with Asher on this one. Should we be worried about a war or something?" Joseph stressed Asher's question to be answered.

"Ok, first there is nothing to worry about yet because the press jumped the gun. We don't even know what happened yet." President Carson replied.

"You can't tell us not to worry when you don't even know what is going on!!!" Both Asher and Joseph hesitated, "We could be on the verge of world war three, and our president does not know!!!"

"Ok, first, there is nothing to worry about. We already told you two this. Second, the President probably thinks we are nuts now." Simon said.

"Well, if we are done with that, let us move on to the tour." President Carson chuckled.

"Hey, can I walk with you four?" Blake asked.

"Sure, but don't you have anything better to do?" Oscar answered, puzzled.

"Nope, I am grounded from all tec," Blake replied. "Why? Did you fail a class or something?" Asher asked sarcastically.

"Or something. I hacked a closed server." Blake answered with his arm behind his head.

"Oh! Wow, you can hack. That is so cool." Joseph exclaimed. "Thanks," Blake said.

As the class walked inside Vice President Linna came out on her phone in a hurry, only to pause for a second.

"President Carson, please talk to Cassie about her people skills. I think they need some work." Vice President Linna said, covering the speaker on her phone.

"Will do Linna," President Carson said, and continued to lead the class into the white house.

A helicopter was waiting on the front lawn with a man from Dr. Juno's laboratory.

"So, how is the progress going on plan Monarchy?" Vice President Linna asked as she shut the door of the helicopter.

"We are ahead of schedule thanks to Juno's super cure she has been working on. What about her brat that caught us a few weeks ago? Will he be a problem?" the man answered.

"No, he wouldn't be a problem at all." Vice President Linna said, with a slight smile, "Pilot, we are ready to leave now."

"Oscar, what is it?" Joseph asked, grabbing Oscar's arm to catch his attention.

"That is the man I was telling you guys about. The one who was snooping on mom's computer." Oscar said, watching intently as the helicopter left.

"Wait, the guy that was in the file for the super cure?" Asher asked, shocked.

"Yes, that is him. Blake, is that man her bodyguard?" Oscar replied, still watching it.

"I don't believe so. If he is, he does a horrible job at it." Blake stated.

"Hey, you boys might want to keep up." a gardener said, walking past the door.

Later that night, Vice President Linna had met up with two men. The first is a tall muscular man with blond hair and blue eyes, dressed in a German military uniform. His name was Kazeimir. The second man, clothed in a Russian military outfit, is short and thick, with black hair, brown eyes, and a scar above his left eye. His name was Charles.

"This had better be important, Linna. We still have tests to run before the release." Charles remarked.

"You should be done with the lab rats already. We are ready for phase two and have been waiting on you, Charles. Everything relies on those precious lab rats you had to have." Kazeimir said.

"No one is allowed to act without my permission unless you want to end up in a grave. Now I said to take you time with the lab rats because one slip up and Juno's brat son might put two and two together, or Juno's super cure would reverse our bioweapon. Second, if you are not careful, Kazeimir, President Carson will catch you, or his son will." Vice President Linna scolded them.

Right then, a man walked in that was 5'6", slim build, wearing a black suit, aviator sunglasses on, and had black hair, carrying a sniper rifle.

"So, who is the target? By the way, I expect to be paid half of my cost up front." the man said, looking around.

"You are late, William. If you are late now, how can I trust that you will put our plans into motion? After all, gaining control of the US is riding on your shoulders? It has to look like another country tried to assassinate the president, or it will come back on us, and if that happens, they will not be the one to hunt you. I will, and you will die slowly and painfully." Vice President Linna warned.

"Understood now about my payment?" William replied, "With it being a country leader, I want 30 grand upfront and 50 grand after I shoot him. My only question is, why do you not want me to kill him right off the back? wouldn't that be less risky than a poison bullet that the doctors might find?"

"That may be true, but I need him to send Cassie to Mrs. Queens academy. Then Blake will be sent to Officer Cobie. I need those two separated for the plan to work, and the only way that will happen is if President Carson thinks his kids are at risk. There is one more issue to cope with: your nephew got himself into a pickle on his mother's computer and now hanging out with Blake. The two of them together is a problem." explained Vice President Linna.

"So, when do you want me to take the shot?" Questioned William.

"As soon as the virus is ready." Vice President Linna dismissed them and walked out.

A week had passed, and Blake was still in contact with Oscar, and the other boys were trying to figure out what Vice President Linna might be hiding. They tried to talk with their parents, but without proof, no one was interested in hearing what they had to say. The only one outside of the five boys that was convinced she was hiding something was Cassie. The only difference was Cassie had a feeling it was something awful. The closer it got to the dad for monarchy to start, the more careless Vice president Linna got because she knew the five boys couldn't figure out how to bust her. Little did she know Cassie was watching her every move, listening to every call, recording it all, waiting for Vice President Linna to slip up.

"President Carson, have you thought any more about the academy I suggested? I honestly think it will be good for Cassie. Plus, I know someone that might be willing to help with the hacking problem you have with Blake." Vice President Linna suggested, holding the papers for the academy.

"I don't know. Cassie does not like to hang around people that often. Then I don't think Blake learning better ways to hack is a good idea. He could accidentally hack another country's missiles or worse." President Carson started to dismiss the idea.

"Well, what do you expect when you have always home-schooled your children because you have been a politician since Cassie was born. She has never had the chance to socialize with any kid her age. As for Blake, he has gotten into a lot of trouble because of his skills. I think it might be best if he has something to do with it. After all, it might help save a few lives. At least think about it." Vice President Linna pushed for him to send them away, not saying the real reason why.

"I guess there is no harm in looking into the ideas a little more like you said it might be good for them."

President Carson agreed and walked away while reading the paper for the academy.

When Vice President Linna's phone rang, she walked to a shed that was hidden from view.

"Hello. Yes, he is thinking about it. After he sends them away, we will be able to release the virus to cause enough panic in order for us to take over and make new laws here." Vice President Linna answered the phone, unaware of the fact that Cassie was listening.

"My nephew has nothing on you. So, there is nothing for you to worry about. Everything will be ok as long as his friends and Blake don't find you. So tonight, for the shooting?" William asked.

"Yes, tonight. For their own protection, he will be willing to send them away after the press conference. Plus, Dr. Juno is still at least a month away from finishing her super cure, so as long as she does not know that the virus we created is from her research, there is no way to stop us." Vice President Linna said, sounding so sure of herself, as she hung up the phone.

After hearing what she just heard and having it recorded, Cassie knew she had to stop Vice President Linna somehow, but first, she had to warn Dr. Juno about the Virus. She hurried to find Blake and take him with her because she couldn't hear what the person on the other side was saying, and she didn't want to risk it being something awful.

"Cassie, what's going on? Where are we going? Where are the guards that we were supposed to have? Wait, Cassie, are you thinking about driving?!" Blake asked with concern.

"I will explain on the way. We are going to Dr. Juno's Lab. We can't trust anyone outside of dad in the white house, including our so-called guards, and yes, I am driving! Now hurry up and get in." Cassie answered, starting the car.

As soon as Blake got in and closed his door, Cassie sped off to warn Dr. Juno.

"Okay, Cassie, now tell me what's going on?" Blake asked again. "You and your friends were right about Vice President Linna. I have a recording of her talking to someone on the phone. She minced something about a virus made from the cure she has been working on. We have to warn Dr. Juno." Cassie said, flying down the highway.

"Cassie, even with the proof without knowing who else is on the other end. They could still release the virus and we would not know who." Blake replied.

"I know this, but maybe if we warn Dr. Juno, she might be able to figure out who else is involved and create a cure for it." Cassie pointed out, speeding up some more.

"Ummm….Cassie's dad is calling. Did you tell him where we are going?" Blake asked, holding up the phone.

"No. Hit talk and don't say anything," Cassie ordered. "Okay," Blake said, hitting talk.

"Cassie, where are you and Blake? The gardener said he saw you taking one of the cars without a driver or any guards." President Carson questioned her.

"No need to worry, dad. We are just going to see Dr. Juno's son.

Blake asked me to take him to see his friends because the guards make them nervous." Cassie responded quickly.

"Okay, next time, please tell me. What friends?" President Carson replied.

"Umm... The four from the tour you did a couple of weeks ago. You know the ones worried about World War Three." Cassie said, "Sorry for making you worry."

"It's okay, next time tell me. Bye, sweetie, love you guys and be careful. Stick to the speed limit, Cassie. I mean it." President Carson added and hung up.

"Cassie, you lied. You told dad we were going to see my friends, but we aren't." Blake said.

"Blake, I know, but if we tell dad, then what happens, we need this conference to show Iran that we are not scared." Cassie answered.

As they pulled up in the parking lot, Cassie unbuckled and flung the door open, and took off into the lab with Blake close behind her.

"Dr. Juno are you here???!!!! Dr. Juno!!!" Cassie came into the main doors yelling.

"Cassie??? Blake???? What are you doing here?" Oscar asked, puzzled.

"You were right about Vice President Linna. We need to warn your mother now." Cassie said, looking around the entire lab.

"She went to get takeout for dinner. She will be back soon." Oscar informed them.

"Ok, well, give her this, tell her she has to listen to it. It is a recording of Vice President Linna talking to someone. We have to go. Dad has a press conference, and I have a bad feeling about it." Cassie said, grabbed Blake by the wrist, and left.

"Will do be careful," Oscar replied, watching them race outside.

As Cassie and Blake turned on to the road for the white house, the press was already lining up to meet with the President. They had traffic backed up so much it was bumper to bumper with no room to open the car doors. Horns were honking left and right with angry drivers yelling and cursing because of it.

"Cassie. Now, what traffic is at a standstill?" Blake asked, looking at her to answer.

"Come on, we need to get out of the car." Cassie said, rolling the window down and pulling the key out of the ignition.

"Wait!? What?" Blake replied.

"You heard me. Vice President Linna mentioned something about tonight. Come, we can climb out my window." Cassie responded, halfway out the driver side window.

"Cassie, that is a mile run easy and a lot of people. With the threat, we received from Iran this morning. I don't think it is a good idea." Blake pleaded with his sister.

"What threat?" Cassie asked, startled.

"No one told you. Someone threatened the white house staff, saying that they were members of an Iranian terrorist group." Blake informed her.

"Still, that could be what Linna was talking about. Now you can come with me or stay in the car that is not going anywhere due to traffic. It is up to you, but I am going to that press conference. So, if you are coming, better hurry up." Cassie said.

"Ok." Blake replied

They both took off in a dead run, weaving between the cars stuck in traffic. Once they reached the main gate, they had an easy 700 people to get past. Little did they know William was already in place waiting for Vice President Linna's order. As they finally reached the front of the crowd, a red dot appeared on President Carson's chest. Before anyone knew what had happened, he fell to the ground, and his shirt quickly turned red with blood.

"Dad!!!!!" Cassie screamed, as she started to shove people out of their way.

"Dad, hang in there!" Blake pleaded, picking up President Carson's head.

He was quickly rushed to the hospital by chopper.

"We have a gunshot wound. Though and though. I want a C.T scan and X-rays to make sure there are no life-threatening injuries." a male doctor said, "Did I stutter? Now would be nice!"

The Doctor was about 5'6", on the slimmer side, and had green eyes with dark brown hair.

"Yes, sir." a resident replied, filling out the paperwork to get him in the O.R.

It was an hour later when Cassie and Blake had heard anything.

"Sir, it has been an hour since our father went in for surgery. I demand to speak with someone as soon as possible." Cassie demanded.

"He is out of surgery, young lady, and will be fine. President Carson is in recovery and wishes to speak with you now." A female nurse replied.

The nurse was wearing pink scrubs, white tennis shoes. Her hair was blond, and she had green eyes. The nurse walked them down a long hallway with the elevator at the end of it. The walls were white, the floor was white and gray, and there was a door every six feet on either side. At the end of the hall was the door to their father's room.

"Dad, how are you feeling?" Blake asked.

"I am ok, Blake, but I would like to talk to you two." President Carson said, looking at Cassie.

"Why did you not one tell me about the threats made against you? Or why would you still have the press conference knowing this? At least wear a bulletproof vest. You could have died." Cassie exploded, staring at him.

"Cassie because we did not think it was nothing to worry about." President Carson answered, waving for her to come closer to him and Blake.

"We! We who?! That is what happened with mom because no one took that threat seriously, and now look at what happened as a result. So, we, who?!" Cassie yelled.

"The guards and Vice President Linna. Now please calm down so I can talk to you both." President Carson replied.

"Wait, you did not have a bulletproof vest because Linna said it was nothing!!!!!!" Blake yelled, turning to look at his dad.

"Yes. Now both of you calm down so I can talk to you." President Carson said.

"Fine." Cassie and Blake both answered.

"Cassie, you will be going to an academy for your safety and to learn better people skills. Blake, you need to say bye to your friends because you will be going with officer Cobie to learn how to improve your skills. This way, you both are safe and will learn some much needed skills." President Carson told them.

"What? No way in hell, I will go to some academy that Linna suggested!" Cassie yelled, "Her last idea could have killed you!"

"I agree with Cassie!" Blake jumped in.

"That is enough. You are both going. The threats are coming more often and you two have a habit of acting before thinking. So, you are going for your own safety.

Today was a fine example of that, you should have had guards with you, but you took a car and left. Then left it in the middle of the road and ran to the press conference. You both have until the end of the week to have everything ready to go. I don't want to hear any ifs and buts." President Carson said.

Cassie waited for her father to fall asleep then went looking for Vice President Linna.

"What do you mean it was the wrong bullet? How can it be a plain one when the only ones you have are covered in poison?" Vice President Linna asked angrily over the phone.

"If I knew that I would tell you. Maybe someone switched them. Hell, if I know what happened." William replied.

"It is lucky for you that Carson is still sending his little brats away. So, everything is proceeding as planned. We just need a new way to off Carson." Vice president Linna said.

"If you don't mind me asking Vice President Linna. Why do we need the brats out of the way?" William questioned.

"Because they are a big enough threat to us with it just being one of them, but both of them can for sure expose our plans. That is why we need them out of the way." Vice

President Linna said, hanging up the phone and stepping out of her car.

"Vice President Linna. I have been looking for you." Cassie snapped.

"Yes, Cassie? How can I help you?" Vice President Linna asked.

"You told my father not to wear a bulletproof vest after he got a threat on his life!!! What in the hell is wrong with you! Then you convince him to send Blake and me away!!!!! I am not dumb. I know you are up to something!!! We hear you on the phone talking to some unknown person. You just want Blake and me out of the way!!!!" Cassie snapped, "Stay away from my family."

"I think we are done here, Cassie." Vice President Linna said and walked away.

After that, both Cassie and Blake went home to pack, and hopefully, figured out a plan to finish busting Vice President Linna.

"That does it. Blake, I need you to hack her phone. We need to know where the super virus is being created and who all is involved." Cassie whispered.

"Ok, will do. What's it matters if we get into trouble over it now. If we don't do anything now, something terrible could happen." Blake said, opening his laptop.

"Any intel we find gets sent to Dr. Juno. She will want to know, and they will listen to her better" Cassie said.

33

Chapter Three

Outbreak Contained

"**M**om, here is the rest of what Cassie and Blake sent," Oscar said, handing her a printed map on where the super virus was being created.

"Ok, Oscar, I will be back. I am going to see what is going on at this other lab. Just in case you need to go to Asher's house and stay the night. Your father is leaving with his class for a science fair in Missouri. So please stay out of trouble." Dr. Juno replied.

The lab for the super virus was secluded from the city. It was in the wilderness, with the nearest house was four miles away. The road to get to it was a five-mile-long gravel driveway. The driveway had big green trees on either side of it, and at the end, the lab had a chain-link fence all the way around it. On top of the fence, there were three rows of barbed wire to keep the human lab rats. Dr. Juno parked her car just out of sight then walked up to the edge of the fence to avoid being seen. She sat in the brush pile, taking pictures of everything she was seeing.

Right then, two men in hazmat suits outside carrying a dead woman, with a rash and blood coming from her eyes. This confirmed that what Cassie and Blake had been sending her for the last week was true. Now there was the problem of stopping it from spreading to the rest of the country. She took pictures of them throwing the body into a large hole filled with bodies. None of the patients had survived past two hours.

"We don't get paid enough to keep packing dead bodies back and forth." the man in the blue hazmat suit said, looking in the hole at all of the dead bodies.

"I know, but if we quit, they might just turn us into a human lab rat." the man in the yellow suit replied, walking back in.

Dr. Juno started to look for a weak spot in the fence as soon as the two men went inside. Then she found a hole just big enough for her to fit in. A few plants and a tree obscured the crater.

"How am I supposed to do anything with this if they will not survive the drive to the city? They need to survive at least 24 hours." Vice president Linna said calmly, walking outside to go to her car.

"Well, madam, we are trying, but the virus is two deadly. To do anything like that, we need more time." a man about 5'4" with round glasses replied, shaking so hard he almost dropped his clipboard.

"First, it was the human lab rats, then that idiot naive Dr. Juno! Now it is more time! I will give you one week before I decide to turn you into one of these lab rats!!! Am I clear, you poor excuse of a scientist!" Vice President Linna yelled, slamming the door to her car.

The scientist picked up the papers he had dropped and rushed back inside to try to find a patient that would survive for a complete 24 hours. After he went in, she crept over to the windows to get some pictures of what was going on inside the building. What she saw would horrifying for anyone to see. There were people crammed into cages too small for them to stretch out. Then there were five strapped to beds waiting for the scientist to inject the virus in them. Ten men were wearing hazmat suits waiting for the other five people with the virus to finish dying. The last thing she saw was a woman in a glass box that looked sick but did not have the rash or bleeding from her eyes like the others were. The men all called her patient zero.

Once Dr. Juno knew it was safe to leave, she crept back to her car and slowly drove away.

"Oscar, I need you to stay at Asher's for a while." Dr. Juno said, leaving a voicemail on Oscar's phone.

When she got back to her lab, she printed off all of the pictures she had taken and made a copy of the video of Vice President Linna talking to the scientist about the virus. Then she placed it with the stuff that Cassie and Blake had sent her. Then she hid it in Oscar's bag, which he had forgotten there. After that, she installed Blake's virus on her desktop so that the computer they were using to steal her research would catch it as well; as soon as the virus took effect, the desktop began to emit sparks. While that virus was doing its work, Dr. Juno started to shed the paper copies of her research. The last thing to do was find a way to stop the virus from spreading.

"Vice President Linna, can you come back to the lab? I think! We may have found a lab rat that will work, and the computer is dead. I think one of the idiots was using it. But that is ok because if this works, we will not need it anymore." the scientist said over the phone.

"Great, I will be there tomorrow night." Vice President Linna replied, "How long has that one survived?"

"This makes 24 hours, and she is showing no symptoms of the virus. I will be placing her with some of the others to see if she is a carrier for it." the scientist answered.

"That is great. If anything happens before we send her to the city, move her to our prison pod on the island. Am I clear?" Vice President Linna replied.

"Yes, Madam. I understand completely." the scientist said and hung up the phone.

Little did either one of them know that Dr. Juno was on her way back to the super virus lab to set it ablaze in order to stop the spread of the virus.

Dr. Juno snuck back around to the hole she had found earlier that day. Once she was inside the fence, she used the wiring to cause an electrical fire. Then she dumped gasoline all over the ground and building, so it would burn faster and kill the virus before the fire department arrived there to put out the fire.

Once the building went up in flames, she dropped a match on the gasoline she had dumped around the building. As Dr. Juno was leaving, she failed to notice the scientist who left with patient zero. They both climbed into a black car and sped out of there leaving everyone else to burn to death.

"This better be good for you to call me an hour later after giving me an update." Vice President Linna said answering the phone.

"Well, madam, you may want to consider plan B. I have patient zero with me now, but the lab was set on fire." the scientist replied.

"Ok very well then, plan B it is." Vice President Linna said, hanging up the phone.

It was an hour later when Dr. Juno wrote a letter and placed it in Oscar's bag, then put it under the desk at the main entrance. After that she turned on the only working on the computer and set it up as a live video stream for everyone to see.

"Hello, my name is Dr. Juno Willis Smith. I have to say something, and everyone needs to hear it. There is corruption in the white house. A select few stole my research and were trying to create a super virus with it. I'm not sure how high up the corruption chain is, but it simply means that we, the people, must become aware of what is going on around us. I have stopped the virus from leaving the only lab I had found, but there might be more.

Our own government is corrupt by greed and power, and the corruption is caused by." Dr. Juno said right as Vice President Linna unplugged the computer.

"You just could not help yourself from digging, could you? Well, I can't have you messing up our plans." Vice President Linna held the cord in her right hand, "Take her to the prison pod and make sure no one knows what happened to her."

"You will not get away with this." Dr. Juno said.

"But I already have my dear doctor." Vice President Linna said walking out of the door to the lab, "Oh! Yes, thank you for jump-starting world war three for me. You just saved me some work."

"Wait, you did all of this to start another world war? What in the hell is wrong with you? What would you benefit from this?" Dr. Juno asked, puzzled.

"Power, control, the country. You see, this virus was supposed to wipe out some of the population, allowing me and my partners to take the United States." Vice President Linna, "But you made my job a lot easier. So, thank you again."

After that, two men took Dr. Juno to the same prison pod where patient zero was being kept. The prison was located in a Florida swamp.

Chapter Four

The Beginning of WW3

"Sir, Germany just fired a missile at our embassy in London, and Russia fired at Hong Kong." a man that was 5'6" with black hair, brown eyes, and a black suit on.

"Wait, what?" President Carson asked, hanging up the phone. "Sir, we are on the verge of another world war." the man said.

"Well, that was just the Mexican Embassy in the United States. I fear you are right. Dr. Juno's video has caused nothing but chaos. Please let me know if someone finds her. I need to know about whom she was talking about." President Carson replied, rubbing his head.

Suddenly an energy newscast came on every T.V. There had been an attempted assassin on a cabinet member. The streets began to fill with panic behind the new reporter. People were running in all directions, cars were piled up, and the fire erupted everywhere. The wreckage was exploding with cars. Behind the reporter, emergency vehicles' sirens could be heard. Wires were broken and hanging in the streets.

"President Carson, this might be a bad time to tell you, but Iran had just declared war on Australia." Vice President Linna said, looking at the T.V.

"Great, can someone please find Dr. Juno? We have no choice at this rate; we have to act." President Carson replied, waiting for the bad news.

"Sir, your son, is on the phone." a lady wearing a maid's outfit said while passing President Carson.

"Ok, thank you, Sue." President Carson replied, grabbing the phone, "Hello Blake is everything ok there?"

"Hey, dad. Yes, everything is ok. I was calling to check on you." Blake answered.

"We are ok here, but I think you might be safe to stay with officer Cobbie." President Carson said.

"Ok, I guess I can. You need to go see Cassie as soon as possible." Blake replied.

"I know, but I think it is best to let her cool off. I believe that she is still mad, so I am sending Vice President Linna to check on her with everything going on and to make sure she is safe." President Carson said.

"You are sending Vice President Linna instead of going yourself?" Blake asked.

"Well, Vice President Linna volunteered to." President Carson replied, "I have to go, Blake. Bye, love you, and stay low."

Vice President Linna arrived at Mrs. Queens academy a few hours later to check on Cassie and see if she had begun to obey orders.

"Still, isn't she listening to anyone?" Vice President Linna asked.

Mrs. Queens was 5'6" with a slim build. Her hair was black and in a tight librarian's bun. Her eyes were blue, and she had thin black glasses on. She was wearing a long black skirt, a white blouse, a black jacket, and black heels with white stockings.

"No, she is not listening to anything I have to say. I have had her here for two and a half weeks, and I have had no progress, and to make matters worse, she is hanging around another girl just like her. How am I supposed to break her if she is so bullheaded and will not talk to anyone except Rosetta. I have tried everything that comes to my mind. We are on to holding food until she obeys what I say." Mrs. Queens replied.

"You better think of something. I need her brainwashed into obeying our every order." Vice President Linna said.

"I know madam, Would you like to speak with her? Maybe she might be more willing to listen if she speaks to you." Mrs. Queens suggested.

After Vice President Linna spoke with Mrs. Queens, she walked through the halls. The walls were a light gray, and the floors were white and black tile. There were no pictures up anywhere in the classrooms; there were four rows of desks with six in each row, a green chalkboard, and the teacher's desk. She finished walking through the class hallways after 20 minutes and made it to the dorms. The dorm rooms had; gray walls, white floors, the door and window frames were black, there was only one bed and desk in each room with a small closet large enough for seven uniforms. When she did not find Cassie inside, she checked the yard. The yard: had a nine-foot-tall fence going all the way across from one wall to the other, barbed wire on the top of the fence as well as the bottom and middle of it to take the option to try and escape away. And the grass was yellowish-green, and there was a plain dark green metal table bolted to slabs of concrete. Underneath the oak tree Cassie sat there reading a book about prison escapes.

"Cassie, there you are, I have been looking for you everywhere, young lady." Vice President Linna said, standing in front of Cassie.

"What do you want now?" Cassie asked, glaring over her book.

"Your father had asked me to check up on you with us being on the verge of a world war three. Mrs. Queens has also informed me that you are still not obeying anything she says." Vice President Linna replied, looking at Cassie's book cover, "Surely you are not going to try and escape. You are much safer here than outside of these walls right now."

"You can stop wearing that mask; I know this war is all your doing, the hitman who shot my father was hired by you, Dr. Juno's disappearance was also your doing, and the virus was your plan. You knew that if Blake and I were in the same place, we could expose you and your allies to the true demons they are. So, you can stop the fake ass shit already because you can't fool me." Cassie remarked, standing up to look Vice President Linna in the eye.

"Okay then, since you figured it out, allow me to point this out. If you dare to get in my way, I will have you join Juno. So, you better think very carefully before you do anything stupid. Oh yes, obey Mrs. Queens like a good young lady. Am I clear, Cassie?" Vice President Linna replied and started to walk away.

"NO! Those who want to create chaos will never get my respect. I will uprise and rebel against them and fight for what is right. I do not fear you, and I will never obey Mrs. Queens. I promise you I will escape, and I will expose you for the devil you are. So, try your best to stop me." Cassie snapped, staring at Vice President Linna as the shock started to appear on her face.

"Good luck Cassie. You will need it because no one has escaped the academy, and Mrs. Queens has broken everyone she has had in her school. You are no different. You will obey one way or another." Linna simply replied as she went inside.

"So, is she going to listen now?" Mrs. Queens asked, and Vice President Linna walked to the entrance.

"No, she is not. She is going to fight you every step of the way. You need to break Cassie because she is resourceful and knows everything. So do what you must, but make sure she obeys every order" Linna said, walking to the car, "Oh! Yes, Mrs. Queens."

"Yes, madam?" Mrs. Queens answered nervously.

"If you fail me, I will kill you slowly and painfully." Linna warned as she closed her door.

After that, Vice President Linna drove her black car to a helicopter and went back to D.C. only to see that more chaos was breaking out. There were protesters on the streets in front of the

white house. The police continued to try to assist them, but it had little influence on the crowd, which was far more than the police office. Across the street, people were fighting over race. Everything was going just as Vice President Linna had planned so far. The only problem was Cassie knew everything and was not going to break as easily as she had thought.

"Vice President Linna, how is Cassie? Is she still mad at me for sending her there? Has she made any friends yet?" President Carson asked, meeting her at the helicopter.

"Oh yes, she says hello. No, she is not mad at you anymore, and I told you it would be good for her. She has made a few friends already, plus Mrs. Queens said that Cassie is her favorite student there. However, I do have some bad news for you. Sadly, she is not allowing any student to leave or any visits until this war is over for the girls' safety. I apologize because if I had known that this was the last visit, I would have sent you to go see your daughter." Vice President Linna replied softly.

"Well, I guess it makes sense since one of them could be severely injured if she does not lock the school down until the war is over. Better safe than sorry. At least she is making friends." President Carson said, dropping his head.

Weeks had passed, and things were just getting worse worldwide. President Carson was hoping that this would not lead to nuclear warfare. Blake was helping officer Cobie in the German embassy while Cassie was trying to find a way to escape the academy with the help of her friend Rosetta. Slowly the weeks began to turn to months, and things were not improving for anyone, including Mrs. Queens, who was not getting anywhere with Cassie and was back tracking Rosetta.

"Look, President Carson, what if we get some of the counties to sign a treaty?" Vice President Linna asked knowing, he would say no.

"The only treaties that have been offered is for Russia and Germany to take part of our country. I will not dare allow that. Plus, that will not help the chaos in our own country. We may be fighting two wars and losing both but handing over our country to the people who started this conflict is not an option. Do not ask that again." President Carson dismissed Vice President Linna's suggestion.

"Yes sir." Linna replied and left the room.

Meanwhile, Oscar snuck into his mother's lab, hoping to find anything to show him where she might have gone. The only thing he had found was a messy lab, distorted files, and his bag he had forgotten that night. It is what was in the bag that said it all. It was all the evidence proving that Vice President Linna was behind it all and the name of patient zero. Plus, the name of the virus, along with what it was supposed to do and last was a letter his mother had left him.

Dear Oscar,

In case I don't get to tell you in person, I am so proud of you. You have grown up so much in the last few weeks. The courage it took to prove what you and your friends had found out was correct. Now it is my turn. I have stopped the virus from ever getting to the public. Now I must expose Vice President Linna for the real devil she is. Listen to your father and trust your friends, because if I fail, it will be up to you seven to make things right. I love you and am so proud of you, Oscar. You are my little Odysseus. Be strong for your father. You both will need each other.

Love, from,

Mom.

That was the first thing Oscar read in the bag. After that, he told Simon, Asher, and Joseph to meet him at the old skatepark in an hour.

"Oscar, what is it?" Asher asked, looking at Oscar, who was standing under the ramp.

"Yeah, it is not like you just to send us a text to meet and not say what for." Simon jumped in, confused.

"Hang on, we are waiting for Joseph and because I could not risk someone else reading the text." Oscar explained.

"Hey, sorry I am late, it is a farther walk to avoid the protesters. So, what is going on?" Joseph asked, catching his breath.

"I went to my mother's lab to try and find anything to help find her, but I found this instead. It is the evidence to prove Vice President Linna is the guilty one. Along with the info about the virus and the origin of the test subjects. All of them were from that plane crash a few weeks before everything. The virus is called Echidna, the mother of all viruses. Like from Greek mythology. They did have one successful patient named Elizabeth A.K.A patient zero." Oscar said, handing them the file, "I don't know where my mom is, but she left a letter saying that it was up to us, six kids, and my dad. So, we need to find Blake and Cassie as soon as possible."

"I was right, the plane was the start of world war three. I told you all, but it was only paranoia." Asher remarked, as he passed the file to Simon.

"Asher, I think you are missing the point. Is it really the time for an 'I told you so'?" Simon replied, looking up from the file.

"Oh! Correct, sorry, wrong time." Asher said, looking at the ground.

"You were right, but now we have a problem we must solve before things worsen." Oscar said, placing his arm on Asher's shoulder, "together we stand."

"Quick question: the world is in world war three, and the United States might as well be in a civil war, at the same time; how can things get any worse than what they are?" Joseph asked, looking around at the guys waiting for an answer.

"Dude!!!! Why in the world would you ask that?! Things can always get worse when you ask that!!!" the other three yelled.

Right then, they heard an explosion from down the road. The boys took that as a sign, all left for Oscar's house for the night. Not sure how to tell Robert what was going on but knew they had to. On their way to Oscar's house, Asher's father passed them, going in the direction of the explosion they had heard ten minutes prior. After they watched four more cop cars pass, two fire trucks, and three ambulances pass, the boys figured it would be best to pick up the pass.

Chapter Five

Fallen Leader

It had been a year and a half since World War three started. There was no sign of it breaking any time soon. To make matters worse, the United States was still suffering from all of the riots that had started the first few months after the war had started. The rioters kept targeting hospitals, police departments, smaller stores, courthouses, even peaceful protests against the war. The crime rates were growing as well; there were at least 20 murders in two days from a single town, innocent people were being mugged for their belongings, cars were being vandalized left and right, houses were being set on fire.

With Blake being at the Russian embassy, he was unable to leave until the war was over. At the academy, things weren't getting any easier for Cassie and Rosetta. Mrs. Queens was determined to break both of them. In the meantime, Oscar and the boys were doing everything they could to help in the reconstruction of the homes that had been destroyed in the commotion. Robert Smith brought food and medicine to hospitals and safe houses that were still standing. Despite everyone's efforts, nothing seemed to be working. It was like they got three steps forward and to a giant leap back.

"Sir, with all of the riots going on, I don't think you should be giving a speech. These rioters are becoming more dangerous, and only a week ago, another cabinet member was hospitalized. Please cancel it." Alexander Smith said, holding a bulletproof vest.

Alexander was 6'2", with a slim build. His hair was black, and he had brown eyes. Alexander had been the one to help President Carson after Cassie's mother was killed. Cassie's mother was Alexander's half-sister, but he never had the chance to tell any of them. After some days, he thought it might be best to let it be and focus on Cassie and Blake.

"Alexander, I know that you are worried, but I think it will be fine. I will have to do one sooner or later. At least this way, I might be able to calm our county down some." President Carson replied, as he fixed his tie.

"Ok, fine then, at least wear the bulletproof vest. Don't forget the last time you choose not to wear one. I will not be the one to tell them that you got shot again because you did not wear it. They would find out from the T.V. Do you really want that?" Alexander pointed out, holding up the vest for President Carson.

"Ok, you have made your point. I will wear it. I never had the chance to thank you for being there for us after all these years." President Carson replied, putting on the vest.

"Well, don't. You guys are the closest thing I have as a family." Alexander said, looking at the floor.

"Well, I will thank you for everything." President Carson said, walking out the door.

"You are welcome. You fool, be careful. They don't need to lose another parent." Alexander said, following him out.

The front lawn was filled with press crews waiting for the speech from the President who allowed corruption in the white house. Outside of the fence were about 35 protesters and cars covered in graffiti. Little did he know William was in a building across the street.

"Hello, as you all know, these are troubling times, but we can't stop this war by starting a civil war. We need to rise up from the ashes and stand as one united as a county. I know that fear has taken over and allowed this evil in, but I ask you as an equal to help find the light. We will find the one behind this corruption and bring them to justice. That will do no good if we do not change what we are doing to our country. Those who are fighting two wars cannot win either war. So, I ask you, does this violence need to be continued until there is nothing left to fight? The only way we can change is to help those who cannot help themselves. One person can make a change no matter how small it may seem, but a bunch of people standing as one can cause a revolution. The world needs to change. We all know this, but violence only causes more violence. We must confront violence with compassion. The problem with the old saying and eye for an eye, is everyone ends up blind. So, I am asking you all to stand as one and join me before we have no country to fight for." President Carson said, standing at the podium, hoping his speech would help stop all of the riots.

The entire time William was waiting for President Carson to finish his speech as ordered, but before he could fire the shot, he received a call from Vice President Linna.

"Wait before you shoot him. I need you to make it seem as if it was rioters. This will keep the heat off of us. There is a group of rioters headed that way now. There are about 200 of them, so it will be easy to lose any cops in the crowd, and they wouldn't know who did it." Vice President Linna instructed.

"Yes, madam. Just keep in mind my fee to kill him." William said, looking at the rioters that were coming up on the street.

"Do you see them yet?" Vice President Linna asked.

"Yes, I see them," William replied, lining the sights up.

"Wait for the riot to start, then take the shot." Vice President Linna said and hung up.

Suddenly, the rioters started to throw Molotov on the lawn. Then their attention was turned to the crowds of people on the streets trying to flee the scene. Some of them even attacked the press vans and cars in the streets with sled hammers and crowbars. While all of this was going on, William aimed and fired at President Carson's head, knowing that he had worn a bulletproof vest. President Carson hit the ground with no warning for the people standing close by. He had been shot in the head. With President Carson dead, William carefully packed his belongings, taking care not to leave anything that might tie him to the murder of the President.

"Carson! Damn it, Carson, don't you dare die on me! Fight. You can't die yet. You have to stay with me. Please, for Cassie and Blake's sake, don't die! They can't lose you too. Please stay with me. Assistance is on the way." Alexander yelled, kneeling beside him, not knowing what to do.

They rushed him to the nearest hospital, but President Carson had already died by the time they reached.

"Blake, I have some bad news for you." Officer Cobie said, walking in holding his hat.

Officer Cobie was 5'6" with a muscular build. He had short brown hair and brown eyes.

"What is t sir?" Blake asked, standing up, knowing it was bad news.

"I am sorry to be the one to have to tell you, but one of the rioters shot your father. He did not make it." Officer Cobie replied, placing his hand on Blake's shoulder.

"What?! No, it can't be! You are lying! Vice president Linna put you up to this!" Blake snapped and stepped back, shoving Officer Cobie's hand away.

"Fine, if you don't believe me, turn on the T.V. See for yourself; I don't blame you for not believing what I say." Officer Cobie said, handing Blake the remote, "But I am sorry."

"No." Blake said, dropping the remote in shock.

"Blake, I am sorry." Officer Cobie replied and started to walk out.

"Does Cassie know?" Blake asked with tears rolling down his cheeks.

"Pardon me?" Officer Cobie asked, turning around.

"Does my sister Cassie know?!" Blake snapped.

"I don't know. The academy doesn't have T.V. there, I am unsure. So probably not." Officer Cobie answered.

"Well, I want to go tell her. She will not believe anyone else." Blake said, wiping the tears from his face.

"I am afraid you can't. First, for your own safety, you are not allowed to leave. Second, the academy where Cassie is locked down until this war is over." Officer Cobie said, walking out of the room.

It was about two days after President Carson had died. Today Vice President Linna became the president. Everything was going as planned, minus the fact that Cassie still had not broken yet and was becoming more rebellious towards Mrs. Queens. She would soon change that, or so she thought.

"Cassie, report to my office now." Mrs. Queens said over the intercom.

"Now, what does that old hag want? You go ahead, Rosetta. I don't think we are in trouble this time." Cassie said changing directions to the office.

Rosetta was 5'2" with an average build. Her hair was long and brown, and her eyes were blue.

Cassie was covered in bruises and cuts from Mrs. Queens and the consent escape attempts. When she walked in, she had her head held high and was ready for a fight.

"What did I do this time, Mrs. Queens?" Cassie questioned.

"Nothing Cassie. I am here to tell you that rioters had shot your father after a press conference." President Linna said and stepped toward Cassie.

"I told you to drop the fake bullshit. If he is dead, it is your doing not the rioters. You already made one attempt on his life. You are here to tell me you are President now. I know that. I will make sure it is not for long, you devil. I will get out of this hell hole even if it is the last thing I do, but I will expose your true colors." Cassie snapped, storming out of the office.

"Young lady, get back here and apologize to President Linna for your behavior." Mrs. Queens said, stepping into the doorframe.

"Kiss my ass!" Cassie yelled, from the end of the hallway.

Little did President Linna and Mrs. Queens know they had sparked a dangerous fire with Cassie. Now all bets were off; she was going to escape even if it meant burning the academy to the ground. Her father's death signaled the start of a conflict.

"Cassie, what are you doing? It is daylight now; they will catch you." Rosetta asked, looking around for guards as she grabbed Cassie and pulled her off of the fence.

"I have to get out of here. Linna had killed my father, I have no clue where my brother is, and she is the President now. I know I might get caught, but I must try before things get worse." Cassie explained, looking back at the fence.

"Wait, how does your father's death have anything to do with Linna becoming President? Wait, President Carson was your Father. Oh, Cassie, I am so sorry." Rosetta said, looking at the fence, "But we still need a better plan."

"Ok fine, we will figure out a safer way. Then we will put an end to President Linna's rule." Cassie said, walking inside with Rosetta.

"No, I will not sign the treaty yet. If I do, it will look suspicious. So, I will sign it in about three to four-month.

That way, they will think that I am doing what is best for the country." President Linna said, talking to Kazeimir over the phone.

"Ok, madam," Kazeimir replied, and hung up.

After that phone call, she had called Officer Cobie to see if there was any progress.

"Officer Cobie, has Blake completed the task as you asked?" President Linna asked.

"Yes, for the most part. You were right; he does have a talent for hacking." Officer Cobie replied.

"Good, at least one of Carson's brats is obeying what we tell them." President Linna remarked.

"So, Mrs. Queens has not broken Cassie yet?" Officer Cobie asked.

"No, that incompetent fool has not. The more she pushes, the more Cassie pushes back. Mrs. Queens has tried everything that has broken girls in the past. None that works with Carson's brat." President Linna answered.

"Well, it is not like she is a threat." Officer Cobie tried to point out.

"You dumb ass. She knows about everything!!!" President Linna snapped.

"What I meant was no one has ever escaped the academy, and Mrs. Queens has broken every student to go there." Officer Cobie replied.

"That was the case, but Cassie made a friend. With the two of them, they might get out." President Linna said.

"Ok, what about Dr. Juno's son? Does he know anything?" Officer Cobie asked.

"That damn doctor says her son doesn't know a thing, and it appears he doesn't." President Linna replied.

"Well, then that is one less problem we have to deal with." Officer Cobie remarked.

"Yes, it is." President Linna responded.

"Is patient Zero still alive?" Officer Cobie asked

"Yes, she is. Now I must hang up. I have an appointment in Florida." President Linna said and hung up.

Chapter Six

Hell in the swamp prison

President Linna had pulled up to a ferry to go to the prison pod that she was keeping Juno and patient Zero. The water was a green color caused by all of the algae. As the ferry passed all of the trees and logs, you could see the crocodiles' head pop up out of the water. There were boats in trees and trash floating everywhere.

Once the ferryman pulled up to the dock, the chain-link fence was the first thing they could see. The fence was an easy ten-foot-tall with three rolls of barbed wire at the top, and the inter fence was electric. The prison was a small gray stone building with no windows and two metal double doors, one double door for the front and the second for the back. The inner area for the pod prison was surrounded by quicksand and swamp water. The only way out of the prison was the ferry that came once a month with food and supplies for the guards.

The guards' living accommodations were merely a bed, wardrobe, couch, stove and fridge, and a T.V within the building, which had white walls and iron bar doors every 12 feet. The scientists in charge of patient Zero came next; they were similar to the guards, but they had medical equipment. Then was the kitchen to prepare the food for Juno and patient Zero; this had running water, a stove, fridge, microwave, a washer and dryer in it. The prison cells were where they had kept Juno and Patient Zero; the cells were bulletproof glass with air filters in them, there was a single twin-size bed in each cell with white sheets and a pillow. President Linna made sure to keep Juno and patient Zero at opposite ends of the cell area.

The back room was designed to torture anyone who was places there to obtain information. An electric chair, a metal bed, chains dangling from the ceiling, live rats in tin cans, and a cabinet with whips, torches, rags, and a few ball pein hammers, as well as a metal chair with wrist and ankle shackles, were all in this chamber. The temperature in this chamber was regulated at 32 degrees Fahrenheit. Blood was splashed all over the floor and walls.

President Linna shifted her gaze to Dr. Juno. This was a signal to take her to the rear room to be interrogated.

"No, please! No, I have already told you everything!" Dr. Juno pleaded with her.

"You know, when people are being tortured to death, they tend tell fewer lies. I need to make sure no one else knows about me and my partners." President Linna said, running her index finger along with a few hammers, "Put the Doctor in the metal chair, make sure to strap her down and put the gag. I don't wish to hear her scream. Last chance Juno, did you tell anyone else about this."

"No, I did not tell a soul." Dr. Juno pleaded once more, "Please don't do this."

"Fine, have it your way." President Linna said, slamming the hammer into Dr. Juno's left pinkie, "How did you find the lab? Did someone tell you?"

Juno shook her head no. Knowing that if she said a thing, Robert, Oscar, and all Oscar's friends would be tortured or killed. President Linna kept at it until she ran out of fingers on Dr. Juno's left hand.

"William, take Dr. Juno back to her cell. I will give her a week to think about whether or not she wants to tell me what she knows." President Linna ordered her, "Now I must go clean up before I leave."

"Yes, madam." William replied, walking into the room, "Hello, my dear sweet sister-in-law. It has been a while."

"William, please, you have to help me get out of here." Dr. Juno said as soon as he removed the gag.

"You don't understand, do you? I am not here to save you. I am being paid a large amount of money for each job I do. So no, I will not help you." William said.

"You are helping that she-devil! For money of all these things! Robert was right about you. You are no good trading family for money." Dr. Juno snapped, quickly slapping him with her right hand.

"Maybe you should have thought about that before you chose my brother over me, sweetheart," William said, pushing her toward her cell.

"You were a hired hitman killing for the fun of it, and when you weren't killing, you were drinking. So, I know

I made the right choice." Juno replied as he shoved her in the cell.

"Tell me, do you know who Oscar's biological father is?" William asked, looking at her waiting for an answer.

"It is Robert! Stay the hell away from my son!" Juno yelled, hitting the glass.

"Goodbye, Juno," William replied with a smile.

"I want a DNA test done on the doctor's son, but make sure no one knows." President Linna ordered the scientist.

"Yes, but if you don't mind me asking. Why?" the scientist replied.

"Just curious. I think the bot might be of some use to us." President Linna responded and left.

Later that night, a guard came with Dr. Juno, and patient Zero dinner. He was wearing a yellow hazmat suit. They had peas, plain rice, a cold bologna, and a glass of water for dinner. When he got to the door, he opened a small sliding glass window just big enough for the tray to fit.

"Wouldn't it be easier to talk?" the guard asked, passing Dr. Juno's tray.

"No, it wouldn't be because I am the only person who knows." Dr. Juno replied, grabbing her tray.

"If you say so, but no one believes you. We all know that you are lying; someone else knows." the guard said, "It is only a matter of time before you talk."

"I will die before I say a word." Dr. Juno replied.

"Whatever you say, doctor." the guard said and walked away.

After that he walked down to patient Zero. Her hair was black, green eyes, and was pale. You were not able to tell how tall she was because she sat over in the corner. They made sure that she had extra food and clean clothes. She didn't even appear sick. She showed no symptoms of the virus, but the last two people she was with had caught the virus and died within 72 hours.

"Here you go, patient Zero." the guard said, placing the tray on the glass, "Are you going to talk to me today?"

When she did not answer, he turned around and walked back up the hallway.

"Maybe if you try her real name, she might talk to you. Then again, why would she talk? You infected her with a virus that kills anyone who gets within three feet of her, not to mention you are holding us against our will." Dr. Juno remarked, sitting on her bed.

"We are doing nothing wrong. All we are doing is cleansing the world. There are too many people on the earth. Only the fittest will survive when we are finished." the guard said, staring at her through the glass.

"What the hell is wrong with you people?" Dr. Juno asked. "Nothing is wrong with us. It is just the natural order of things.

You are weak and will break and anyone else who knows." the guard said and left.

As the days passed, the guards gave Dr. Juno less and less food and water. Finally, a week had passed, and President Linna returned to torture Dr. Juno some more. President Linna had walked down the hall without saying a word. She opened the door to the backroom and walked in and began to hum. As she ran her fingertips along the chair debating what method of torture to use. Finally, stopping at the metal bed with restraints. President Linna began to fill up a bucket of water and hum again. Once she had four buckets filled, she signaled for them to bring her into the room and strap her down.

"Last chance Juno, tell me who else knows about my plan." President Linna said.

"Go to hell. I am the only one who knows." Juno said, spitting in President Linna's face.

"Get me the rag. You will talk easily, or I will break you into a million little pieces, and then you will talk."

President Linna replied, dumping water on her head as two guards held the rag on her face.

After two buckets of water, she had them remove the rag, giving her a chance to talk, but she refused to. After that, she used the last two buckets, but Juno still would not say a word about who else knew. Then she looked over at a metal box that was in the corner.

"Put her in the freezer for a bit. Maybe she will talk after we allow her ill-mannered self to cool down." President Linna said, walking out.

They left her in the freezer for about 30 minutes before they let her out. When she still refused to tell them who else knew, President Linna picked up a whip and gave her ten lashes before sending her back to her cell. The two guards dragged her back to her cell while President Linna walked behind them, still humming.

"I will allow you to think about your choice for another week." President Linna said and walked out.

William was waiting at the ferry when President Linna had walked out. The look on his face implied that he knew President Linna was up to.

"Why did you have a DNA test done on Oscar, Robert, and Me?" William asked.

"Well, you asked Juno who Oscar's father was." President Linna replied.

"Ok, then what did you find out?" William asked.

"Oscar is your brother's son," President Linna lied.

"Ok. Thank you for checking into that for me." William said, walking onto the ferry.

"You are welcome." President Linna said with a smile and walked onto the ferry.

Chapter Seven

End of one War and the start of a new war

"President Linna, it has been a year, sign the treaty or not, but this war needs to stop. If this war does not end, we will both lose our countries. Your country is extremely close to another civil war. Therefore, you should sign the treaty now, and we will help restore order, or another country will invade and take over, then there goes the plan." Charles pointed out over the phone.

"I know. I have to make sure that it was not going to seem suspicious. Now is the time to sign it. It will appear as it was the last option that we had. Listen to me closely, though. If you or Kazeimir dare, try to double-cross me there will be severe consequences." president Linna replied and hung up the phone.

Later that week, President Linna called a press conference to announce the United States signing a treaty with Russia and Germany. She had William and Alexander on either side of her. She also had the security increased around the white house.

There were only ten news crews there to avoid chaos. Every guard was armed, snipers were looking out for any sign of trouble, plus the police all had either bean bag launchers, live rounds, and rubber bullets. President Linna was wearing a bulletproof vest and had a small nine-millimeter pistol. There were paramedics on sight in case of an emergency.

"I have decided it is in our country's benefit to sign a treaty with Russia and Germany. Now they will be sending troops here, but there is no need to be alarmed. With the recent rise in violence, I believe that it is in our best interest for everyone's safety to set a curfew just until everything returns to normal. I know this may seem a bit far-fetched, but it is for our safety. The hospitals have been receiving far more than their capacity, with 20 people coming in every hour due to just gunshot wounds. You must have a permit on you if you are out after ten o'clock, or you will be detained. I do deeply apologize for the inconvenience, but again this is what is in everyone's best interest in order to help cut back on the violence that has overtaken our country." President Linna lied, knowing that things would not return to normal as long as she remained in power.

As she walked away, William followed her without a word leaving Alexander at the podium to deal with all the news crews. After 30 minutes, the last news crew had finally left.

"Why on earth would you be willing to sign a treaty with the two major countries that started this war?" Alexander asked angrily.

"As I said, it is in our country's best interest." President Linna responded with no hesitation.

"I am having a hard time believing that, but that does not matter." Alexander replied and walked out.

"Are you not going to deal with him? After all, what if he starts to dig as Dr. Juno did? He might become a problem." William asked.

"No, with the former president' best friend at my side makes me more likeable and if I see he has become a problem, I will send him to our land in the swamps to join our dear friend Dr. Juno." President Linna remarked and sent William to make sure that everything was in place for the treaty that she would sign the next day.

The next morning, she had Kazeimir, and Charles meet her in the oval office. This would be the turning point of the country of freedom. A seed of greed had been planted and was beginning to take root.

"So, after the treaty, we will announce it to the world, and if the war does not end out of fear, then we will fire nuclear missiles at the rest of the world, taking out their capitals forcing them into chaos," Charles stated.

"That is the plan, Charles, but Linna, what took so long to agree to sign this part was your plan?" Kazeimir asked.

"If I had jumped to it, the country would have rebelled against it. I had to wait for them to cause more damage on their own. That reminds me, don't either of you two dares think of double-crossing me. If you do, you will regret it." President Linna answered as she signed the treaty, "Feel free to move your troops in as soon as tomorrow morning. Make sure they use their manners at first. The more people on our side at first, the better it is for our plan."

"Yes, madam. We understand fully." Kazeimir responded. "Now, what about Juno and patient Zero?" Charles asked.

"They are in a remote prison, so our secret doesn't get loose."

President Linna answered as they left the oval office.

It was a month after they had signed the treaty when the world war had stopped. President Linna, Charles, and Kazeimir had the troops start detaining all rioters. If they resisted, they were shot in the head without any hesitation. After that, they began to arrest anyone with a criminal record, erected fences around small towns, allowing the guards to leave after dark, people were getting beaten and shot in the streets for speaking out against those who were supposed to protect their freedom, the money was coined, guards set houses on fire to clear out certain spots for headquarters. Rulers were placed on what kind of meat you could sell, and the amount of meat they could purchase each week. As months passed, there were more laws, with harsher penalties for those who disobeyed them. On top of all of that, they took away the bulletproof vest from the police.

Then those three announced that there would be no more elections. Sure, there was order, but only after everyone lost their freedom.

Robert, Oscar, Asher, Simon, and Joseph did what they could to help to make the people's life a little easier; they gave away extra blankets, canned food, bottled water, clothes, and gloves. They made sure to be back at the houses an hour before dark to avoid any guards. The more they helped, the more went missing. One day, an older man looked a guard in the eye. That was when they realized how bad things had gotten. The guard began to beat the older man with a baton once the man was unable to get up, then the guard pointed his gun at him.

"What is wrong with you? All he did was look at you. There was no need to beat the hell out of him, let alone shoot him." Officer Joe said stepping, in front of the older man.

"Eye contact is a sign of rebellion. Rebels must be killed on the spot. Orders," the guard said, "But, I guess I will spear his life. You own this man's family, your life, don't forget that."

With no warning, the guard shot Officer Joe 17 times in the chest. As Asher raced to his father, who was just killed out of cold blood with the other four right behind him, everyone else cleared the streets.

"Let him stand as an example! Speak against us, look us in the eye are signs of rebellion! Now, does anyone else want to test their luck today!" the guard yelled, looking for anyone who would say something.

"It is getting dark, Asher, we have to go now." Robert said, placing his hand on Asher's shoulder, "We will bury him in the morning."

"They shot him for no reason. Since Linna has taken over, every right we had was taken. I swear this is war." Asher said

"They will. Come, stay with us. Also, we should bring him with us, so no one takes his stuff." Oscar said, picking up his feet.

"Ok, thank you, guys," Asher replied, grabbing his father's shoulders.

As they packed Officer Joe's cold lifeless body home, they noticed that they were being followed. Once they got home, Oscar turned around and was ready for a fight. Asher quickly jumped in front of him. It was Blake who was on his way to see them, warn them of the new laws that were coming, and to see whether anyone had heard from Cassie.

"Blake, what in the hell are you trying to do? Trying to give us a heart attack?" Simon mocked.

"No, I was finally allowed to leave the Russian embassy. I wanted to tell you that things are going to get harder. They are getting ready to release new laws." Blake warned, looking around, "Have any of you guys heard from Cassie yet?"

"More laws! Their dumb ass laws just got my dad killed! Something needs to be done about this!" Asher replied angrily.

"Wait, you have not heard anything from Cassie?" Oscar asked.

"Not since she was sent to the academy. They don't let anyone visit or call. The only one that can is President Linna. I don't even know if Cassie knows that Dad was murdered. Sorry, Asher. If there is anything that I can do, let me know." Blake said, looking at the ground.

"Thanks, Blake. We should go in before we get in trouble." Asher said, walking toward the door.

"Sorry, Blake, no one has heard from Cassie." Oscar said.

"I am sure she is fine," Joseph said.

The next day Blake helped them bury Asher's dad before leaving to return to the embassy.

"Your guards killed one of my friend's dad!!!" Blake walked in and yelled at Officer Cobie.

"So what? I am holding the report. Maybe if he had minded his business, he would still be alive. That reminds me, the next time you do not report in, we will have problems. I can't kill you because you are under President

Linna's protection, but I was told to keep you in line, Blake." Officer Cobie replied.

"He was doing his job! You and your asshole guards are to blame for his death! You all say you are protecting the people, but you are just after power!" Blake snapped.

"You ungrateful child." Officer Cobie said, slapping Blake across his face, "You will learn your place, Blake."

Blake fell to the floor due to the force behind the hit. He placed his hand on his cheek and watched Officer Cobie.

Weeks passed, and things kept getting worse. Other countries were unwilling to step in to help out of fear. Then-President Linna started putting people in fields to harvest crops by hand or in buildings that did not get finished because of the war cells were put in them to hold the people sent there to fight for the rich's entertainment. Those were the lucky ones. The rest of them were tortured to death in front of everyone or used as lab rats for whatever purpose needed at that time. It had gotten to the point where no one said anything wrong about the government. Few people were willing to help each other anymore either.

Robert had begun to help break people out with Blake's help to avoid the guards. Robert would sneak them through the woods until he found abandoned houses that had root cellars so they would be able to hide. While Blake sent guards on a wild goose chase through the city, watching them on street cameras and playing Officer Cobie like a fiddle. The other four boys help the people in the city with supplies.

They all kept their heads done to avoid getting caught. Each one was the other's alibi.

"Blake, why have you not found the escaped prisoners or the rebellion helping them?" Officer Cobie asked, walking to the room.

"Sorry, sir, but whoever is helping them is good. They are avoiding all street cams. I don't have access to anything that might help catch the rebels." Blake said, looking at the computer.

"Fine, you can use the satellite imaging and the heat sensor, night version drones. Just catch the rebels." Officer Cobie replied, walking out.

"Sir, it is possible when one of your guards is helping. They are the only ones who knew where my cameras were placed." Blake said to divert attention away from the others.

"This is true. Thank you, Blake. Start watching all of the guards for any odd behavior." Officer William ordered and left.

Blake began watching for any of the guards that could be framed as the rebels. It took him about three weeks, but then the guard that killed Asher's father was caught slipping drugs to a civilian. This is what Blake was waiting on. Plus, the guard was around Asher, Oscar, Simon, Joseph and Robert, which gave them an alibi.

"Officer Cobie, I think you might want to see this. This guard just slipped about ten civilians' drugs and bought some from this man by the brick building barely out of sight. Who is a wanted criminal for; dealing drugs, murder, assault on a guard, illegal firearms." Blake said, pointing at the computer.

"Ok, very nice how many times does this guard report to this part of the city?" Officer Cobie asked.

"Three times a week. Sir, according to the file, he is supposed to be on the other side of the city at this time. Also he has missed checking in once a week for six weeks. That is when the rebels started helping prisoners escape. He might be one of the ring leaders." Blake implied, knowing it was not true because he hacked the systems last night when everyone was asleep.

"Thank you, Blake. I will grab William, and we will go deal with this traitor." Officer William said and left.

It took Officer Cobie and William less than 20 minutes. They nearly hit the guard with the hummer. The streets were empty as soon as the two climbed out. Then another hummer pulled up behind them, filled with guards.

"This traitor is one of our men, go and find that criminal." William ordered, pointing at the officer.

As the other guards went to look for the criminal, William and Officer Cobie shot the guard in both legs and dragged him to the hummer. They tossed him into the trunk of the hummer and slammed the hatch shut, then sped off to take him to President Linna. The other guards continued to search for the criminal. After an hour, they gave up the search and returned to the base to await further instructions. President Linna had told them to find out who else was helping because it was not a one-man job.

"Blake, see if you can find anyone else that might have helped this criminal and traitor. Keep it quiet. The fewer people in the rebellion, the better." Officer Cobie ordered, walking away.

So, Blake started to watch the cameras to see if anyone else had talked to the criminal. There was just one problem: the criminal was no longer there. It had been a week since Officer Cobie and William detained the guard. He decided to use the drones to help find the criminal. The man was hiding in an old building. There were guards coming and going buying alcohol and drugs under the table when they were supposed to be on shift. Blake used this to his advantage for Robert to save a few more people since the guards were too drunk and high to walk. After Blake knew Robert had gotten those people safely, he informed Officer Cobie.

"Is it possible that they forgot to lock the door to the transport vehicle and claimed they had help escaping to cover up the fact that they were drunk and high on duty?" Blake asked.

"Very much so. Good job, Blake. President Linna was right. You are indeed useful. Who on earth thought of a rebellion here of all places?" Officer Cobie replied and walked out chuckling.

Blake had finally figured out how to take the heat off of Robert. The guards, who were too drunk and high to tell which end of the pistol was the barrel, deserves no thanks.

Chapter Eight

Mrs. Queens's Academy Never Gives Up Hope

It had been three months since they had signed the treaty, and things were getting worse. For Cassie, the academy started to seem more like a prison by the minute. Cassie and Rosetta began to study the fence for weak spots but were having no luck thanks to Mrs. Queens's little pets.

"So, I hear that you were trying to escape yet again, Cassie. I told you that you weren't going to escape. Without question or argue, you will obey me, or you will fear me. This is my school, and I will have an order. You are not allowed to cause chaos here." Mrs. Queens said as she smacked Cassie's hands with a ruler.

"I will never obey you. I will escape." Cassie replied.

"Put this young lady in solitary for two days with no food and no water. Maybe then she will learn some manners." Mrs. Queens ordered.

Solitary was a small room in the basement. It was a six by six with light grey walls, a mattress on the floor was the only thing in that room. The mattress was old and hard. There were no windows either. Cassie spent two days in solitary before Mrs. Queens went to talk to her again. Little did Mrs. Queens know that Cassie finally figured out how to get out of the academy. She purposely got caught so she could look at the guard schedule to see when they would be doing room checks and checking the yard. It was only a matter of fooling Mrs. Queens for a few days. Rosetta already knew about the plan and was already playing her hand.

"Do you have something to say, Cassie?" Mrs. Queens asked as she walked into the room.

"Yes, Mrs. Queens. I am sorry for the way I have been behaving. May I have another chance? Please." Cassie replied with her hands placed in front of her.

"Yes, you may, Cassie." Mrs. Queens answered and handed Cassie clean clothes, "Get changed, then report for breakfast."

Cassie waited for Mrs. Queens to contact president Linna. Once President Linna would show up in the morning, Cassie and Rosetta would pretend to be brainwashed. Then that night, they would use the old oak tree to climb over the fence and the other tree to climb down and stay out of sight. Afterward, they will find different clothes to change out of so no one would call the school and report them as runaways. From there, they would find Blake and the others. They had no clue how bad things had gotten.

After two weeks, they finally fooled Mrs. Queens to let down her guard and call President Linna. They showed up to every class, did as the teachers said, spoke politely to everyone, made sure to make curfew, and made sure that their uniforms were ironed and buttoned all the way.

"So, you think you broke Cassie? If you are wrong and if you are wasting my time, there will be a price to pay." President Linna said, walking into the school.

"I believe you will be surprised by her turn around." Mrs. Queens said, walking behind President Linna.

"I will be the judge of that." President Linna replied, walking into the office.

"Cassie, come to my office, please." Mrs. Queens said as she closed the door.

"Game on," Rosetta whispered.

"Yes, headmaster. What can I help you with this morning?" Cassie asked as she opened the door.

"President Linna would like to have a word with you. That is all. I will let you two talk." Mrs. Queens answered as Cassie sat down in the chair.

"Ok, headmaster. I would like to apologize for my behavior for the last few times when you were here." Cassie greeted, holding out her hand to shake President Linna.

"Well, I am impressed. Your behavior has changed so much for never obeying us. If your behavior continues to improve, I will have you move to the training camp for my troops." President Linna replied and sat down.

"Thank you, Mrs. Queens. I do apologize, but I have to go to class now." Cassie said and walked out.

"Ok, you may be excused." Mrs. Queens replied.

After that, President Linna stuck around to watch to make sure Cassie was not trying to pull a fast one on them. Cassie made it to each class on time, was polite to everyone, and obeyed every order given with no argument.

"You might have accurately broken her. Give it another week or so, and I will transfer Cassie and Rosetta to the training camp, but the other seven I was looking at should start packing their belongings. We need more troops that are not going to get drunk on the job." President Linna approved.

"I will have them ready to move first thing tomorrow night. I am going to check on my school for troubled boys. They still need to learn, but I have three that are top of their class waiting for you to pick up. That academy needs a few repairs done; better fences, more security, new windows, window bars, another solitary room, and it is running low on food and blankets." Mrs. Queens replied, grabbing her coat to leave for the other academy.

"Okay, will do. I would like more male troops in return because people fear them more." President Linna responded and walked out.

Cassie and Rosetta waited for room check then slowly made their way down the staircase. Once they made sure to get down the stairs without being seen, they used Mrs. Queens' key card to get outside. They waited for the guard to enter through the side door, then quickly raced to the oak tree. After they climbed up to the branch which was hanging right over the fence they jumped to a nearby tree. Once they were on the other side of the fence, they used ground pepper to cover their scent from the hounds. They used a map that Rosetta took from a guard who had fallen asleep on watch so they could find a creek or river to cross along with a nearby town.

"Cassie, are you sure this is safe?" Rosetta asked, walking in front of Cassie.

"Look, I told you I don't know, but this has to be better than the academy," Cassie replied, dumping the pepper behind them.

"I guess you are right. We should be able to stop and rest soon." Rosetta said, pointing to a grove of trees.

"No, we need to keep going until we cross the creek about two and a half miles from here. We can't risk the dogs finding our scent. So, we must cover more ground." Cassie said.

"But we need to rest." Rosetta pleated.

"I know, but we must cover as much ground as possible before room checks at o 500 hours. So, if you want to rest, we must pick up the pace. Maybe we can find a cave or old shed." Cassie said.

Once they reached the creek, there were still spots that had ice that had not yet melted. At the widest spots, dead trees were lying across it. About 20 yards upstream was a small waterfall. There were animal tracks everywhere, bear, panther, deer, coon, even chipmunk.

After they went through the creek, they traveled about two more miles and found an abandoned farmhouse. It was still in good shape. It was light blue, the pouch appeared to have a few weak spots and dust on the glass. The inside was extremely dusty, the walls were a bright yellow, and the furniture was from about 20 years ago. The railing to the staircase did not appear to be damaged. The first room that they went into was the master bedroom. They found some dry clothes that would fit them. After they changed themselves, Cassie got an idea to make them disappear so the academy would stop looking for them.

"Wait, we are going to do what?" Rosetta asked, puzzled.

"We are going to fake our deaths. We will shred our clothes, make a small cut on our arm for the blood, then ditch them by that shed we passed. This way, they will think we were eaten by animals when we tried to escape.

They will stop looking this way, and we will dump out of our supplies to make it seem like the animals tore open our bags." Cassie explained.

They backtracked about a half-mile to ditch the clothes. Once they did that, they continued for six more miles then decided to rest in an old camper that they had to fight the door open. They rested for about three hours, then packed up and started moving again, still dumping the ground pepper behind them just in case. After about three days of wandering through the woods. Before they happened to stumble upon the street, where Robert was sneaking people out of the city.

"Robert? Is that you? What are you doing?" Cassie asked with Rosetta standing behind her.

"Look, I don't know who you are, but you can't tell," Robert said, calmly backing up.

"Wait, Robert, it is me Cassie," Cassie said, taking off a hat.

"Cassie! You are Blake's sister." Robert said, in shock.

"Yes." Cassie replied, "Where is my brother? Is he ok? What on earth is going on? Why are you sneaking around with all of these people?"

"Blake is safe. As for what is going on, how do you not know?" Robert responded.

"We just escaped the academy. We don't know anything going on outside of the academy walls." Rosetta jumped in.

"Oh! Then we have a lot to catch up," Robert said as he started walking in the direction they had come from.

"Robert, wait, you can't go that way. We were careful, but we might have been followed. So please don't go that way to be safe." Cassie said quickly.

"Where are you going to go then?" Robert asked as Cassie pulled out a note.

"I don't know, but I will not risk my brother's safety. Give him this note." Cassie said, handing the note to him.

"Cassie, I think I should take these people somewhere safe. You go to the city but stay out of sight to help others escape. It will be harder for them to find us if separated in this manner; if they see one of us, they will think we are dead." Rosetta stepped in.

"Ok, but for safety, I am still going to keep my distance from the others. So, more people can find you for help. We will make carvings on the trees, ok." Cassie said, watching Robert put her note in his pocket.

"Ok, so it is settled. This young lady will get you, people, to safety." Robert said, going the same direction he came.

"Rosetta, remember Zig on the hill, so you don't fall." Cassie said, "Till we meet again, Ziggy."

"I will. Stay strong. Till we meet you again, Oakra." Rosetta said, leading the people farther away from the city.

"Ziggy be sure they all change what they are wearing and find new names for their safety," Cassie said and vanished in the shadowy woods.

Weeks had passed, and everyone had their own part to play against the rebellion they had formed. People who were on the run would go into the woods and look for three knife slashes on big strong oak trees. Blake began to gain more access to more tech the more people got their freedom back as long as they stayed the road. Robert broke them out of the trucks and brought them to the wood line.   As for Cassie, no one has seen her since that night, but it was not hard to figure out she was watching out for all of them. Her calling card was usually two to three arrows to the chest, or they had been stabbed with a saber. She only shot guards who had seen one of the others' faces. When the troops were on the move, she took out the truck along with the guards. Even though no one saw her, they knew she was there.

"What do you mean they are dead!!!" President Linna yelled.

"I mean, the girl escaped the night you left. We found their things and clothes covered in blood and surrounded by coyote tracks. That was it." Mrs. Queens replied.

"Well, if there is more escape, we will have problems. Now I have a new batch coming for both schools coming in, and they best be ready in four weeks." President Linna demanded, as she shot Mrs. Queens's foot.

Mrs. Queens began to scream in pain. Blood was on her shoe and also on the ground. The bullet went all the way through her foot and was embedded in a rock she was standing on. Mrs. Queens' blood was splashed across President Linna's' white heels, which acted as a warning.

"Now, don't fail me again." President Linna warned and left.

Chapter Nine

From Town to Pods

After three months, Cassie and Rosetta had escaped; guards started to put chain-link fences up around small towns to keep the archer out. Little did the GR states know that the archer known as Oakra was really Cassie. She had begun to spread out to the other cities and small towns, taking out guards and helping people escape. The fences were put up around low populations so they could put some criminals in until they could be moved to the fields or the pits.

"Look, this town has about 25 acres of good flat land with rich soil perfect for another field. Put a rice field. Then I want a fence and towers around the field and small sheds for them to stay in. make sure the guards are armed." President Linna explained, pointing at an open field.

"Yes, madam. I will have the prisoners start working on it right away. Everything will be ready in a month." a lower-rank male guard replied.

"I want them in chains. If any of them refuse to work, put them in the freezer. The pits are nearly complete. Once they are done, I will have Commander Cobie and Officer William choose some for fighters. So, keep track of the strongest ones." President Linna said, leaving to check more pods to find more field lands.

President Linna ventured to six other plods to find land for the fields that ranged from ten to sixty acres. There were at least seven fields in each sector where prisoners could be housed. There were three sectors, 45 pods in each, and seven field pods in each sector.

The field pods grew various crops like; peppers, rice, corn, cotton, wheat, stinging nettle, black berries. The prisoners were forced to break up the land manually, dig trenches by hand using pickaxes and shovels to prevent flooding, till the rows for the seeds, and plant each seed by hand. They toiled in what appeared to be impossible conditions.

After that, each area had three pits. Only the elite classes had access to the pits, which were located in bigger cities, where they could see convicts fight as they did in Rome. The three chiefs chose the most powerful captives as fighters and the pits in which they would battle. The inmates were forced to struggle over strewn-about pieces of meat. The water they gave had a rusty tint and was full of dirt particles on its best days. Those who refused to fight; spent days in their six-by-six cells recovering from heavy beatings by the guards.

"Ladies and gentlemen, welcome to tonight's event! We have many fights lined up for your entertainment! To start the night, let's welcome! rrrrRocky and his opponent! The one, the only Exterminator!!!!!!!" the announcer yelled into the mic from the pit floor, "Who will win?! The indestructible rock?! Or the undefeated Exterminator?! Let's find out. Let the match begin!"

Rocky was 5'7", native American, with a very muscular build, black hair, brown eyes. He was wearing; black combat boots, torn blue jeans, a grey shirt, and a grey baseball cap.

The Exterminator stood 6'2" tall, with a muscular build, short brown hair, and brown eyes. He is an African

American. He was wearing; aviator sunglasses, a white shirt, black leather jacket, dark blue jeans, and a pair of high-top tennis shoes with red stripes going across the sides.

The fight lasted ten minutes, both evenly matched when an arrow knocked out the lights. Then a fire started in the back near the top seats, forcing everyone to flee the pits in fear.

"What in the hell is going on?" the Exterminator asked, confused.

"I don't know. Faulty wiring." Rocky answered. "Name is Oakra. Follow me. I have already freed the other prisoners. So, if you want to go out, come with me." Cassie answered from the shadows.

"Look, Rocky, I don't know about you, but I am going with the chick holding a bow." the Exterminator advised, running to the door.

"Don't have to tell me twice. I am also coming." Rocky replied, following behind him.

As guards came around the corner, Oakra raised her bow and placed her arrow. Before they had the chance to load their guns and find them in the dark, Oakra shot two of them in the chest and stabbed the third one with her saber. She made sure to move fast and quietly through the building and the city until they reached the wood line.

"Ok, you are out. Watch the trees. Some markings will help you with them. The first one you should find is three-knife slashes on a tree with a hint to the next. Here is some ground pepper. Dump this behind you, find a creek and walk through it and keep using the pepper. That will make it harder for the hounds to track you. Keep your heads down, avoid the roads, and towns now go." Oakra explained and began to walk away.

"Wait a minute, you are President Carson's daughter Cassie." the Exterminator said, grabbing her arm.

"The name is Oakra now. And you never saw me understood." Oakra said, pulling away.

"Wait, everyone thinks you are dead." Rocky jumped in.

"Yes, and it is to stay that way. If they know that I am Alive. Then my brother will be at risk. So, if they find us, we will have problems." Oakra warned and vanished in the woods to the next stop is a field plod and where a bus of kids was being shipped to Mrs. Queens.

"Well, I am not saying anything about it. We will never live it down if anyone knows who saved us." the Exterminator responded.

"Wonder where she is going," Rocky replied, walking into the woods.

Later a white bus was transporting the children to Mrs. Queens academy. The windows had bars going across them. There were seventeen kids, four guards with basic 9mm pistols, and the driver. All the kids were sitting down while the guards were walking around. The tires would be the best bet to make the bus stop and rattle the guards. Oakra fired an arrow at the back right tire. The bus began to swerve due to the popped tire. Oakra waited for the guards to step off the bus before shooting them to avoid hitting any of the children. Once they were down, the driver stepped out and began to fire his Glock into the woods, not knowing if he was hitting anything.

Oakra had already made her way behind him. She hit him with the handle of the saber knocking him out cold. Then dragged him out of the road and led the children off the bus into the woods.

"Follow me," Oakra said, opening the bus door. Oakra leads them to a thicket of blackberry bushes.

She used a stick to move a few of the vines out of the way that was hiding the entrance to an old mining tunnel. This was one of the safest ways to the camps.

"Look, follow this tunnel. It leads to an opening. After that, there is an oak tree with three knife slashes on it." Oakra explained.

She made sure that they got in the mine before letting the vines fall. Then she backtracked, using pepper to cover their tracks until she got back to the road. After that, she went to the other side of the road to lead the dogs on a goose chase. Then used ground pepper to hide her scent, so she could leave without being followed.

"What do you mean that Oakra did this? Who is Oakra? First the archer, now Oakra? What next? How does one person take out five people that have guns with just a bow?" President Linna asked.

"Madam, the Archer is Oakra. We did not see her until she had taken out the guards. By that time, she had vanished without a trace, so I stepped out, but she hit me on my head with something metal. When I woke up, the children were gone." the driver explained.

"So, it is one person causing this much trouble!!!!! I want her found now!!" President Linna snapped.

"Yes, madam." the guards, troops, and diver replied quickly.

"I want more troops on each one of the transport buses. The drivers are not permitted to step out of the bus until all the children are off." President Linna ordered.

"What about Oakra?" a guard asked nervously. "Kill her if you get the chance. I don't want this to happen again." President Linna warned as she stepped into her car.

The next night Oakra showed up at an unfinished field plot. First, she killed the power. Then she took out the guards. After that, she helped the prisoners free. Finally, she fired a flaming arrow into a propane tank, creating an explosion that destroyed part of the field. Meanwhile, the camps were filling up.

"Ziggy, is it? Look, I want to know what I can do to help." Rocky confronted Ziggy.

"Look, Rocky, we can put you on hunting, gathering , or first aid. Blaze can help you with gathering, and Ace can help you with first aid. If you hunt, you hunt in a group and no guns." Ziggy responded.

"I want to help with the rescues like Oakra," Rocky replied.

"No way in hell. Oakra has been doing this for a while and hasn't been spotted by anyone since the night she changed her name. You don't have the skill set needed to do that. If they catch you, they will kill you." Ziggy dismissed Rocky's idea.

"So let me get this straight Oakra is the only person sticking her neck out to free these people. The only one going toe to toe with the troops and guards, and when someone wants to help you say no because it is too dangerous." Rocky questioned.

"Look, if you get caught, it is not just you at risk but also everyone. The answer is no. If you want to help, pick one of those jobs I listed." Ziggy said, walking away.

"No, she is going to need help out there. They will make it harder for her. Oakra will need a team." Rocky augured.

"Ok fine, since you will not change your mind. Then tonight, I will bring you to Robert, and he will help you reach Oakra. If she says no, you do not bring this up again. Do you understand?" Ziggy gave in, "But you will go with the hunting party that is leaving now, we are running low on food, and they need a few extra people to help."

"Ok, thank you," Rocky replied.

"See, if you can't get your friend, the Exterminator might help the party, could use the muscle," Ziggy suggested, walking away.

"Hey, Exterminator, would you mind coming with us on a hunting trip? Ziggy said we are running low." Rocky asked.

"Sure, it is better than sitting around doing nothing." replied the Exterminator.

Once the hunting party left, Ziggy left to check the mine tunnels for more refugees. Who she found caught her off guard. It was Oakra.

"Sorry for so many refugees. We need to talk to Robert and find out what to do." Oakra suggested.

"What do you mean?" Ziggy asked.

"There are too many for this area. We need to figure out something." Oakra said.

"Wait, no one has seen you in three months. Please, come talk with some of these people. After all, you saved them," Ziggy said.

"Not yet. We will meet with Robert and the others tonight. We will need a new plan." Oakra said and left.

When Ziggy returned to camp, the hunting party had brought back two hogs and a few fish.

"Well, looks like you guys did pretty good today," Ziggy said.

"Yeah, these two are pretty good with a spear and knife. Wouldn't mind taking them out for more hunts." the leader of the hunting party replied.

"Well, that is up to them, but Rocky, you are coming with me, Blaze and Ace; you two are in charge until we get back," Ziggy remarked and waved for Rocky to follow.

"Miss Ziggy, would you mind if I came along?" Exterminator asked.

"Yes," Ziggy responded.

They all met up at the edge of the woods. Robert first saw Oakra and Ziggy.

"Ok, so, Ziggy, what is going on? You called us here. We know this is risky." Blake remarked.

"Cool it, Blake. I said we needed to meet. We have to figure out something else. The camp has too many people for that area. So, any ideas." Oakra replied.

"Cassie!!!! Where have you been?" Blake exclaimed.

"I have been staying out of sight. Sorry, but it is for you guys' safety." Oakra replied, "Oh! Blake, it is Oakra now. The more people that think Cassie is dead, the better."

"So, what is the problem with the number of people in the camp?" Robert asked.

"The number of people in the camp is too large. The dogs could catch the wind, the troops might hear them, or someone might stumble on them. We have to figure out a better plan." Oakra answered.

"We could split into groups. Each group goes to a different part of the country. Then we could take in more people that need help as our groups grow, we can slowly make our way back to Washington DC." Rocky suggested.

"No, we can't." Oscar disagreed.

"If it comes down to it, you will. Rocky is right; we need more people who could help us, but let's wait." Robert said.

"I will take the west mountains if it comes down to it," Oakra said.

"Then I will go with you," Blake said.

"No, you are our inside man. We have the upper hand as long as you are there. We need a way to contact you if we do." Oakra said.

"Fine, but you will be taking a group of people with you, so figure out who you can trust," Robert said.

"I will go with you," Ziggy said.

"No, if we have to divide, we will need to have other leaders for each group." Oakra pointed out.

"Ok, so if that is the case who will be the leaders?" the Exterminator asked.

"Oakra, Ziggy, you, and then me. Ziggy and Oakra have the experience, I and you are the oldest members." Robert answered, looking around.

"I will help Oakra," Rocky said.

"What? Look, Rocky, is it? I will not take a chance on bringing someone who is not trained with me." Oakra responds quickly.

"Then train him. Look, he is from the pits that mean he can fight. So that is less he needs to be taught. I will feel much better if you have someone on rescues from now on. President Linna has a kill order on you." Blake said.

"Blake is right. Rocky will be going with you along with a few others from now on." Robert demanded.

"Fine, I will take him and a few others, but I choose them." Oakra agreed.

"Thank you," Ziggy said.

"So, when do we start?" Rocky asked.

"First, I pick the others. Then I see what you guys know. We will go from there." Oakra said.

"Ok, then so it is settled for now each group has a job. Exterminator, you will lead the hunting party, Oakra will lead the rescues, and Ziggy will run the camp. The boys and I will work throughout the city." Robert replied.

"Cassie, wait! Here this is our walkies dad gave us. They only work on this channel and with each other. Take the green one. If you need anything, call." Blake said, handing her one of two walkie-talkies.

"Ok, but Blake, it is Oakra. No one should know that I am alive." Oakra said, hugging him, "be careful."

Chapter ten

Oakra's choice

Oakra spent the next few days training Rocky and watching others to see who to pick. She was keeping an eye on Blaze who was 5'6", a bigger build, with mid-length black hair and blue eyes. She wore pants that were a little long, and she wore a red jacket. The next one was Ace, with 5'2" height, slim build, with short black hair and brown eyes. She was wearing tight black pants with a camo t-shirt. The last one was Yash; he is 5'7", with a smaller build, short spiky blond hair, and blue eyes. He was wearing light blue jeans with a black long sleeve shirt.

Blaze had a few different skills; knowing plants, knot tying, hand to hand combat, and trapping.

Ace had training in; medical, fencing, hand to hand combat, and marksmanship.

Yash's skills were not as useful in a fight but were just as helpful, navigating the land, tracking, basic first aid, and rock climbing.

Rocky only had hand-to-hand combat, but Oakra was going to change that. She was teaching him archery, spear throwing, sword fighting, tracking, and trapping.

"Again, if you get knocked down by them, they will kill you. Now get your ass up and run it again." Oakra ordered, helping him up.

"How many times are we going to run this exercise? We are fighting with wooden swords, for Pete's sake. This is useless. We are getting nowhere." Rocky replied.

"You say useless, but I have taken out a few guards that had guns with my saber. To defeat an enemy, you must adapt. If not, you will end up dead. Now, run it once more." Oakra said, raising her wooden sword.

After a few days, Oakra brought Rocky and the others along with her to another field plot.

"May I ask, how are we going to take these people out of here?" Yash Questioned.

"You and Blaze are staying put. I will have Ace and Rocky come with me." Oakra replied.

"Ok, fine by me, but what is the plan?" Blaze asked.

"We kill the power, then take out the guards. Next, we will free the prisoners. When that's done, we will blow up those gas tanks." Oakra explained.

Everything went as planned until it came to getting the prisoners out. When one of the inmates saw Ace, he committed a murder. He slammed her to the ground taking her knife. While she tried to fight him off, Rocky glazed back to see what the problem was. As soon as Rocky saw what was going on, he tackled the man off of Ace. The two began to struggle back and forth while Ace raced to get Oakra.

When Oakra came around the corner, the prisoner had Rocky pinned on the ground with his hands around Rocky's neck. Oakra quickly released two arrows. Both slammed into the prisoner's back and pierced his lung. He quickly let go, dropping to the ground.

"Rocky, are you ok?" Oakra asked, racing toward them.

"Oakra, there is blood on this knife." Ace reported, pointing at the knife by the two.

"Rocky, are you ok!" Oakra questioned, picking up her pace to them, "You are bleeding."

"I am fine; it is not deep," Rocky replied.

"You still got stabbed. Can you walk? We need to get you somewhere safe before more guards come." Oakra responded, taking off her jacket to apply pressure, then helped him up.

It took them 30 minutes to get back to Blaze and Yash.

"What happened?" Blaze asked, taking off her bag and pulling out a first aid kit.

"One of the prisoners stabbed him." Ace answered.

"Oakra, we have troops coming," Yash warned, pointing at some at the base of the cliff.

"Ok, stay here and keep quiet. If I am not back in ten, leave." Oakra ordered grading her bow and arrows, then went down the hill out of sight.

While the others took care of Rocky, Oakra worked on taking care of the troops. She used the cover of the woods to hide her presence. Then she slowly picked them off one by one from behind. Once she had killed the last troop, she walked back up the cliff side and scouted ahead to make sure it was safe.

"Ok, it is clear for now. Are you good to walk, Rocky?" Oakra asked.

"He should be good to walk, but we will have to watch our pace. If we go too fast and too far, his stitches will tear." Ace answered.

"I am fine," Rocky replied, trying to stand on his own.

"No, you are not. Now sit your ass down and someone will help you. When you get stabbed you are no longer ok. If you try to stand or walk by yourself again, I will shoot you myself." Oakra warned, "Yash and Blaze, you two help Rocky. Ace, you are helping me scout ahead. I don't want to risk getting into a fight with Rocky injured."

"Ok." Ace replied.

It took them about three hours to get back to camp. When they finally got back, Oakra had Ace clean the wound and placed him with a weight limit.

"So, I take it as it didn't go as planned. Was it a guard or a troop that stabbed him?" Ziggy asked.

"Neither. It was a prisoner." Oakra answered.

"Oh, please stick with bringing a team with you," Ziggy replied.

"I have already picked my team. They are all level-headed when things go south. As for Rocky, he needs to think before he acts, but I know he will have our backs." Oakra said.

"So, you are keeping the team that you picked," Ziggy replied.

"Yes, once Rocky is healed, we will start training more," Oakra responded.

After two weeks, Oakra finally let Rocky lift more than ten pounds. Once the stitches were removed, she began training and working with all four. Making sure that each one of them was able to defend themselves when needed.

"I figured you wouldn't want to take anyone with you after the last time." Ace said, picking up a wooden sword.

"I picked each one of you guys for a reason. Plus, the last time was only the first time out, and you all showed me what you were capable of." Oakra replied, spinning her wooden sword, "Face it, you guys are stuck with me."

Chapter Eleven

The City's Gone South

While Oakra and Ziggy were running the camp and rescues, Robert and the boys were helping the best they could in the city. Supplies were running low, and guards were losing their patients with the citizens. Phones were now useless because Linna, Charles, and Kazeimir had placed listening orders on them and began to track them.

"Dad, what time is Simon meeting us with the clothes for the younger kids?" Oscar asked.

"Any minute now," Robert replied.

"Ok, just making sure. There are a few kids that don't have shoes and others that need hats and gloves." Oscar responded.

"Don't worry, Oscar, if you start to become worried, the other two will become worried as well. Then that will not help anyone here. He will be here soon." Robert explained.

Right then, they heard a fight break out down the street. It was Simon and one of the gang members that had been mugging people left and right. About six feet away was a little girl holding a new pair of shoes and her teddy bear. She was crying and screaming in fear. As the guards showed up, the gang member got up and ran away, but Simon was not getting up. The gangster had stabbed him eight times. The boy quickly rushed to check on him, hoping to beat the guards.

"Simon!!! Hang in there! Dad, we need rags. He is bleeding!!" Oscar yelled, propping up Simon's head.

"Here, put pressure on it." Robert said calmly, passing a towel to Oscar, "Well, none of them is life-threatening, so he will be ok as long as it does not get infected."

"Ok, but how do we stop the bleeding?" Asher asked.

"First, we need to get him off of the streets and inside. Then we will have to cauterize the wounds." Robert explained, sliding a tarp under Simon to make it easier to move him.

After they left, the gangster met up with Officer Williams under a bridge down the road.

"Sir, you were right. He has been the one giving supplies out on my streets with those boys." the gangster informed Officer William.

"Good, follow them. I want to know if anyone that they might try to call." Officer William ordered.

"Yes, sir." the gangster replied and left in the shadows.

When they got back to their house, they laid Simon on a bed. Robert cleaned the wounds to remove any infection while Oscar heated the blade. Asher grabbed a rag for Simon to bite down. Once the blade was heated, Robert had the boys hold him down so he wouldn't hurt himself. As Robert cauterized the wounds, Simon began to scream in pain. After ten minutes, Robert had finished perforating the cuts, and it took another fifteen minutes to bandage them.

"He will be fine, but the bandages need to be changed every six hours. Simon will probably be out for a while due to all the blood loss and pain." Robert explained,

"When he wakes up, try to keep him away from getting up. He needs to rest."

"Ok, thank you, Dad," Oscar said, sitting on the floor with Asher and Joseph beside the bed.

Later that night, Robert walked in to change Simon's wounds. Those three had fallen asleep on the floor beside the bed. Simon still laid in the bed motionless.

The next morning, Blake came over to check on them. When Robert opened the door, Blake raced up stairs.

"Blake, wait," Robert said, grabbing his wrist. "No. We need to talk, and all of you guys must know. Before you try getting a hold of the others." Blake explained.

"Ok, but slow down, Simon is still out," Robert said. "You three come here; we need to talk now." Blake ordered.

"What is it, Blake? You normally don't bark orders. That is Oakra's thing." Joseph replied.

"You guys are being followed. Officer William had the gangster stab Simon. In hopes, you will contact Ziggy for help. None of you guys can contact them, or you all will be killed." Blake exposed.

"Well, isn't that great," Simon murmured.

"Simon!!! You're awake!!" the boys exclaimed, racing back into the room.

"So, I have two people to thank for being stabbed," Simon grunted, starting to sit up.

"Whoo, what do you think you are doing? Lay your ass back down now." Oscar demanded.

"Ok, take a chill pill," Simon grunted.

"Look, you were stabbed eight times. You lost a lot of blood and are going to be in pain for a little while. It is better off you get some rest for now." Blake explained, placing his hand on Simon's shoulder to stop him from sitting up anymore.

Later that day, the gangster met Officer William under the same bridge as before.

"So, what do you have for me?" Officer William questioned.

"Not much, sir. They took the kid straight home. The only one to show up was former President Carson's son. That was on the next morning after they cauterized the boy's wounds." the gangster disclosed, "Is it possible you are wrong?"

"No, and I know just how to get it." Officer William snickered.

"How?" the gangster sputtered.

"Commander Cobie's little pet, Blake." Officer William exclaimed, walking away, "Keep watching them, but don't be seen."

"What if I still find nothing?" the gangster asked. "Then we will play my hand instead of yours." Officer William explained.

When Blake denied any knowledge of the rebellion's camp or members, Officer William went to President Linna with a new idea to force the rebellion's hand.

"The rebellion seems to favor the local towns and cities. If we attack one of them, it might trigger them to come into the open." Officer William revealed his plan.

"If you think it will work. I want Oakra dead. Whoever she is, she has been a thorn in my side for almost a year. People will not listen as well if someone is there to save them." President Linna agreed, "Make an example of her and any others you might find."

"Yes, madam. Thank you." Officer William replied and left.

The next day Officer William had 20 troops and ten guards come with him to cause as much chaos as possible. They were setting buildings on fire, shooting innocent people, and arresting the citizens for no reason. All of this was in Oscar's city.

"Stay in; I will be back." Robert ordered racing out the door.

"Well, well, well, Robert." Officer William exclaimed. "William, what are you doing? They are innocent people. They did nothing wrong. Please let them go." Robert pleaded.

"Maybe they are. Maybe not. I am not after them. I want their little guardian angel, Oakra. If she thinks they are in danger, she will come to their rescue." Officer William explained.

"This is wrong, and you know it. Juno would not want this." Robert begged him to stop.

"Oh yes, that reminds me, your wife says hello." Officer William remarked.

"You knew where she was this entire time!" Robert snapped.

"Yes." Officer William smirked as he raised his gun and shot Robert in the chest outside of his house, then glazed at the window to see Oscar.

"Dad!!" Oscar yelled, racing outside before any of them had a chance to catch him.

"Asher, go with him. I will stay with Simon." Joseph hollered.

"Dad," Oscar said, dropping to his knees with tears rolling down his face.

"Oscar. Now is the time to show your strength. You are now their leader. Act like it. You are our Odysseus. It is no longer safe here. Time for you all to leave." Robert muttered with his last breath as all the troops left.

"Ok, dad." Oscar replied while crying, "Time to pack; we are leaving tonight."

"Are you sure?" Asher asked.

"Yes, dad said it was time to leave. We will pack then leave at nightfall." Oscar replied.

"What about the gangster?" Asher asked.

"Let him follow. It is time to change names now." Oscar said.

The two went back inside after they buried Robert. They explained everything that happened. Once they were packed, they left a note for Blake and went out the back. Each one of the boys changed their names; Oscar now went by Odysseus, Asher changed his name to Nightshade, Joseph chose Julius, and Simon went by Saturn.

Blake

Things went south, so we had to leave.

Officer William shot my father. This place is no longer safe, so now it's time to split. We are sorry we don't get to tell you in person. Until we meet again, my friend.

Oscar

They left as soon as dark had come. It took them about three hours to reach the camp due to Saturn's wounds.

Once they made it to camp, Ace bandage Saturn's wounds, and Oakra got rid of the gangster who had been following them.

Chapter Twelve

Time to Split

“Ok, so we will split as soon as Saturn can walk. We still need to figure out who goes with who.” Oakra explained.

“There are too many people for four groups. So maybe we do five. Each group can take four to five people. So, both hunting parties, Oakra’s group, Odysseus’s group, and mine. That makes five groups each with different skill sets to them.” Ziggy suggested.

"That works, but at least one person in each group needs to learn first aid. I'd also feel better if we had a way to communicate with each other so no one shots our own. One is the trees, while the other is the puzzles. We need at least two more." Oakra replied

"Oakra, these are from your brother. There are seven EMP arrows and 30 expletive glass arrows for signals.

He gave them to us almost two weeks ago. He thought you might be able to use them." Nightshade informed her, passing the bag filled with arrows.

"This is it. We have five groups. Each group gets six signal arrows." Oakra replied.

"So, we don't use the arrows unless it is an emergency," Ziggy warned.

"How about animal mimicry," Saturn suggested. "What are you doing out of bed? You should be resting." Odysseus responded.

"He is right. We can use animal mimicry, but yes, you need to get your ass back in bed." Oakra responded.

After a few days of planning, they figured out which director each group would go to, along with the names of the groups and signals to use.

"Saturn, you should not be lifting anything." Ziggy said, taking a bag of medical supplies.

"It has been a week since I've been stabbed. The wounds are cauterized rather than stitched. Every time I've gotten out of my makeshift bed in the last week, one of you has told me to get back in it. The more help you have packed, the faster we can leave." Saturn replied.

"Good, then help pack, but no heavy lifting. Then go to Ace so she can clean those wounds." Ziggy responded, handing him a lighter bag.

Once Saturn had finished helping pack, he went to Ace as ordered. When Ace took off the bandages, she saw that the wounds were beginning to bruise and were showing signs of becoming infected.

"Saturn, your wounds have become infected. You aren't going to like this, but we need to cut the infected ones open. I will be back." Ace informed him, leaving to get help.

"Infected. We have been cleaning it every day." Odysseus questioned.

"So, what do we do about it?" Julius asked.

"Well, that is why I came to get help. I am going to have to cut the wounds open to get rid of the infection. From there, we will stitch up the wounds, and keep him off his feet for a week or so." Ace explained.

"So, we have to hold him down while you cut him open," Nightshade commented.

"Yes, if we don't and he moves the wrong, Ace could hit an artery, organ, or intestine. So, you may not like the idea, but if not, Saturn could die." Oakra explained.

"Wait, where are you going?" Odysseus asked.

"To run an errand if I am not back in one hour, then try it your way, Ace. There is an old pharmacy about three miles down the road. It has been closed for months because the owners were killed. Rocky, you are with me." Oakra replied and grabbed her bow and sword.

"Is that a normal thing with her?" Nightshade asked after she left.

"Yeah, at least someone went with her this time," Ziggy answered.

"What does that mean?" Nightshade asked.

"Well, before, she wouldn't take anyone with her. Now she has been taking four others with her most of the time. This time the other three have their hands full, so that leaves Rocky." Ziggy explained.

It took Oakra and Rocky fifteen minutes to get there. The pharmacy was a brick building with white and blue paint. The windows were cracked but not broken. The door cracked when they opened it, while the doorbell fell off and hit the floor. The shelves were filled with medicine and covered in dust. Oakra and Rocky began to fill their bags with medical supplies. After ten minutes, they had both bags filled and left. They made it back to the others in 45 minutes because they took the long way back to camp.

"Here, give him some to make him sleep and to lessen the pain. You will still have to restrain him, but this should help," Oakra explained.

The following morning, Saturn woke up to the sound of a lady screaming.

"What is going on, guys?" Saturn asked, getting up.

"Hey, what are you doing out of bed?" Yash asked, stopping him from walking out of the tent.

"I heard a scream," Saturn explained.

"It was a panther on the outside of camp. Now get back in bed." Yash demanded.

"Ok. When are we leaving?" Saturn asked, sitting back down.

"Once Ace gives you the all-clear. Until then, you don't even think about getting up. If Odysseus or Oakra catch you up out of bed, they might shoot you themselves. So lay back down. Trust me, Oakra went for a three-mile walk at night in 45 minutes for medicine, so you didn't feel much last night." Yash warned.

"Ok, I am laying down," Saturn replied, laying down as Yash went back outside.

After two days, Ace gave the all-clear for Saturn to get out of bed but told him not to lift anything or move around too much. This is where their fears came true. The troops found the camp, which forced them all to flee. They all grabbed their gear and ran. One guard saw Saturn struggling to keep up with the others and pointed the gun at him. Oakra tackled the guard, not thinking about the small cliff on the other side of him. The two tumbled down the side of it.

"Oakra!!!" Ziggy yelled, staring at the bottom of the cliff.

"Ziggy duck!" Ace yelled as she shot one of the Guards.

Oakra awoke to see the guard standing above her while things were going south at the top of the cliff. She quickly struggled to get to her feet as he swung the butt of the gun, hitting her in the head. As Oakra fell back to the ground, she saw a jug of gasoline. The jug was about half full. Oakra grabbed the jug and threw it at the guard, soaking him in gasoline. Then Oakra lighted a match and threw it on the guard, soaking him in gasoline. While he screamed and yelled in pain, Oakra climbed her way back up the cliff to join the fight.

"We can't run until we make a bent in them," Rocky said, shooting a troop with a revolver off of one of the guards.

"If we leave them alive, we won't be able to run very far, and they will track us. Send a massage." Oakra, replied as she pulled herself over the edge.

"Oakra, you're alive!!!" Ziggy yelled.

"I told you guys, you're stuck with me," Oakra replied, as she stood up and fired off an arrow that went through two guards.

After 20 minutes, they killed all, but one guard. The one that rolled down the cliff with Oakra and caught on fire. Two of the groups had a chance to run without getting into the fight.

"Are you ok? I saw you go over the edge." Saturn asked.

"I am fine. Just some cuts, bruises, and a sprain, but I am fine." Oakra answered.

"Well, don't you ever do that again," Rocky replied.

Before they part their ways, Ace bandage Oakra and the others. Along with cleaning Saturn's wounds.

"So, it is settled, we will meet in two years. After the groups reach ten people, we split the new ones up again, unless the place is safe." Ziggy reminded them.

"Yes, until we meet again," Oakra replied, and they all went their separate ways.

This was the turning point. They were no longer the same scared little kids they had been four years ago.

They were going to return the land to the people who had originally owned it because this is the land of the free not the rich. Greed had taken over, and it was time to band together and uproot it.

They would regroup in two years with enough people to fight back. Until they meet again, there would be hell to pay. This war is far from over.

Chapter Thirteen

Westward

To anyone who is reading this, my name is Ace. I have been traveling with Oakra and a small group of rebels. We were there in D.C when everything went south. To keep everyone safe, we were forced to split up. It has been one year now. Along the way, we have been building the rebellion, but we make sure we do not have more than ten people. So, it is hard for the War States to find us. Up until now, we have been staying in the Rocky mountains. We hope to build an army to put a stop to Linna's unjust rule. This is worse than what happened during World War Two. Every country that was allied with the United States has abandoned us. Hawaii and Alaska have split off from the mainland. We are on our own here. If you find this and wish to take a stand, look for the hidden messages, but if you choose to use this letter to try and stop us, it will be the worst possible mistake you could ever make. You have been warned.

ACE

"Ace, leave the letter in the cabin. We have to get moving." Oakra ordered.

"Yeah, I know." Ace replied, placing the letter on a maple table and weighing it down with a book.

"Why do we even leave these damn notes, Oakra? It seems pointless to leave them." Rocky questioned.

"Look, if anyone comes through here and if they are trying to hide from the War States. This way, they know that they are not alone, and we might get some help later on." Oakra explained, looking back at them.

"That may be true, but it is also a risk. What if a troop or a guard finds one of these letters?" Rocky asked.

"That is why we don't place any intel that could lead them to us." Ace pointed out.

"There is a 50-50 chance either way, but we are the rebellion. We are already taking a lot of risks challenging the government. So, what does one more small risk hurt anything?" Yash replied.

"Fine, as long as we are not leaving one at every stop," Rocky responded, grabbing his bags.

"There is only one in every other town. So, you can relax about that." Blaze remarked.

After leaving the cabin, they went deeper into the mountains. As the time was running, the sun started to go down. They found an old barn that had begun to lean to the left. Up at the top of the hill sat a farmhouse. It looked as though it had caught fire recently. The chimney had fallen over a little and the outside was charred. Once they were inside, they saw that the walls were black, the air was filled with the stench of charred wood, you could still taste the smoke, and ash covering everything.

"This will have to work for the night," Oakra responded, looking around the front room.

"I think it would be better to set up camp in the barn Oakra. At least it has not caught fire." Rocky replied, walking back to the door.

"The barn is unstable. It could fall at any minute, but the house is only burnt around the chimney, so as long as we don't use it, we will be fine." Oakra augured.

"No, this house is not safer than the barn!" Rocky yelled.

"Rocky, Oakra, there is a small cabin in the back. I think it might be the best bet." Yash jumped in.

"Ok, show me," Oakra replied, turning to Yash.

The cabin was small, and the door's hinges were rusted and appeared as if it would fall at any minute; the air inside was stale and smelled as if something had died inside.

"How do you know that stench is not a dead person? Yash, please tell me you guys checked for a body." Rocky questioned, covering his nose.

"Yes, we checked for a body. We only found a dead rabbit. So, I can assure you no one died here." Blaze replied.

"There. If you still want to sleep in the old leaning barn, go ahead, but we will not dig you out." Oakra chuckled.

"Fine, but can we please leave the windows open. This smell alone can kill us." Rocky replied, opening a window, "At least for a little bit."

"Sure thing, big baby," Yash remarked.

"Yash, you don't have any room to talk. You opened the door and threw up." Ace chuckled, walking past.

While they were letting the cabin air out, Rocky and Yash went hunting. Oakra, Ace, and Blaze went to find water and began to dig a hole for the fire so the smoke would travel along the ground and not the air.

"Yash, what are these tracks?" Rocky asked, pointing at a bunch of animal tracks.

"Which ones?" Yash replied.

"Those ones. They look like deer tracks," Rocky responded, pointing at a small group of tracks.

"Those are hog tracks. It might be close if you want to follow them. They are fresh." Yash answered.

"They look like the newest tracks here. So sure, why not." Rocky replied.

They were unable to find the hog, but they killed a few squirrels and some fish. As they reached the edge of camp, Oakra, Blaze, and Ace stopped them. Seven guards were searching the camp. After an hour of hiding, the guards finished the search and left.

"The guards are traveling in larger groups." Blaze pointed out.

"I know, but that means we are making Linna and the rest of the War States nerves," Oakra replied.

"We have to be more careful from now on," Rocky responded, looking at the others.

"I know. We will stay here for the night. Then we will move first-day break." Oakra responded.

"I agree. Who will take the first watch?" Ace replied.

"I will. In two hours, I will wake up Blaze." Yash answered. "Ok," Oakra responded.

The next morning the five decided to start to make their way back toward D.C. The road back would be a long trip.

Oakra's Journal

9/13/2024

When this first started, I thought I didn't need any help, but as time went on, I realized I was wrong. To stop the people in power, I need more than an army. I need the Rebellion, my new family. Together we stand for freedom and protect the people. To avoid being recognized, I cut my hair that night once we knew we were safe. There are times when I miss Blake, but I know he is safe while still helping us. President Linna thought she had won this war, but she was dead wrong because we realized we had to fight for our home. It has been almost two years since that fateful night when we separated. We started off helping people find safety. Now they have chosen to help us fight this war against the War States. This is the land of the free, not the land of chaos and power. This is our home, and it is time to take this fight to them. I believe it is time to leave our land because it belongs to the people, not the corrupt government that has taken over. We will win this war.

Cassie

Chapter Fourteen

Helping Hand

The streets were quiet with hardly any people. In front of a fruit stand, stood a little boy who was an even 5', with a small build, brown hair, and hazel eyes. He was wearing a blue jacket with a gray hood, a black shirt, oversized blue jeans and a pair of old tennis shoes that the bottoms were coming off.

"What is your name, little boy? Don't you dare look me in the eye, you rodent! You better be lucky I'm in a good mood. For that, I will remove a hand, little boy. Come now, you will be an example to anyone who wishes to rebel against us." Commander Cobie exclaimed.

Cobie was one of the top troopers for the War States. To be, he is the commander.

"Please, commander. Please, I promise, I will not do it again! Please, let me go. Help! Someone, please, help me!" the boy pleaded with commander Cobie.

"Commander, I heard a woman screaming down the street, the door is locked! She was screaming for help and crying! I tried to get in, but I can't please go help her! I told her I would go get help. Please help her quickly! You must help her. You must! Please, Commander." Blaze yelled.

"Why should I?" Commander Cobie asked.

"You will be a hero, and they respect you." Blaze replied.

The second Commander Cobie left, and Blaze grabbed the boy. Blaze grabbed his arm and started dragging him behind her.

"Come back here, or I will kill you both for rebelling! Do you two hear me?! All troops, we have runners! Catch them and kill them!" Commander Cobie yelled, "one male traveling with one female, whose description is long black hair, blue eyes, long jeans, red jacket and is about 5'6! I repeat, catch them and kill them!"

After running for five miles through the woods, they swam through a small river and started to zig-zag through the woods once more and began to dump pepper behind them so that the hounds could not track them down as easily.

"Can we stop running now? I am tired?" the boy asked.

"No, not at all until we reach camp. What is your name, kid?" Blaze questioned.

"Luke," the little boy replied, "Why would you help me? They will be looking for you now. What is your name? if you don't mind me asking?"

"It's Blaze. Come on, Luke, we better pick up the pace if we are going to get there before dark." Blaze answered.

It was almost sundown when they both heard a baby's cry behind them. They were being stalked by a panther. The panther was about 30 yards behind them. It sounded as if it was hiding in a grove of trees. So, Blaze picked up the pace but made sure that it didn't seem as if she was running to avoid the panther chasing them.

"What was that? A baby? Why did we speed up a bit?" Luke whispered in terror.

"That is not a baby; that is a big cat which will kill us if we are not careful. So, stop talking and keep walking. We have one mile until we reach camp." Blaze said quickly and quietly.

After 20 minutes, the big cat left. Within ten minutes, they reached camp. It did not take a rocket scientist to see that Rocky was irate about Blaze bringing an outsider into camp without warning.

"Blaze, one-minute please. Red, guard the boy." Oakra said.

Red was a four-month-old red heeler wolf mix and waist height on Oakra. His coat was shaggy with a reddish-brown tent.

"Yes, Oakra." Blaze responded.

"Who is he, and why did you bring him here?" Oakra asked. "Luke is his name, and he is ten years old. I brought him here because Commander Cobie was going to cut off his hand for looking him in the eye. That is why. I hope this is ok with you, Oakra." Blaze answered.

"That is fine, Blaze." Oakra replied, "Rocky, he is one of us now. Can one of you two show him where he will be sleeping, please, and thank you?"

"Oakra, there is a big cat not far from camp." Blaze pointed out. "OK, thank you for the heads up," Oakra responded.

"Who is the lady with red hair, green eyes wearing black and white clothes?" Luke asked Rocky.

"That is Oakra." Rocky answered, "Now get to bed."

Right then, a guy with blond spiked hair, 5.7 with a smaller build, came out of the woods dragging the panther behind him with a 17 mag on his shoulder.

"Hey, Rocky, it is your turn to skin the meal," Oakra said, pointing to the panther that the guy just pulled from the wood line.

"Yash, it is nice to see that the panther didn't eat you, and you got us some dinner home," Rocky remarked.

"Yes, I got dinner, and I also found an old beat-up farmhouse. It looked like it had about six rooms. Plus, it has a spring-fed creek and a well." Yash said.

"That is great news. Hey, have you seen hiccup or Ace?" Oakra reasoned.

Hiccup was a black and brown mix breed that was six months old.

She was knee height. Oakra had found the pup when she was eight weeks old.

"Ace is at the lookout tree, and hiccup is downplaying in the creek about two yards from the camp. So, are we staying here at camp tomorrow, or are we moving to the farmhouse?" Yash said.

"We will leave at dawn," Oakra answered.

The next day they started to pack quickly to get to the farmhouse before the storm hit. They made sure that both dogs were upfront with Oakra and Yash. The Blaze's bobcat was in the middle with Luke. Meanwhile, Rocky and Ace scooted ahead to make sure that no War State troops were waiting for them. By the time they reached the old farmhouse, they were soaked to the bone.

The farmhouse was a light blue, the trimming and porch were a dirty white, the windows were boarded up, the screen on the storm door was torn, and the chimney was in perfect condition. Twenty yards away was a red barn with a tin roof that was missing sheets. The fence had rotted in certain spots and fallen.

"I'm cold," Luke said.

"We will get wood, and a fire will start to dry off and warm up." Ace told him.

"It is storming, so the troops will not be able to see the smoke," Rocky remarked, looking at the dark sky as lightning broke across the sky.

"Before we do anything, we need to have a look around the place. So split into groups, ok." Oakra said.

Within five minutes, they had checked around the house and made sure it was clear. Rocky and Yash made a fire while the others worked on finding dry clothes upstairs. They also found some money to get food and supplies. Because of the treaty with Russia and Germany, paper money was no longer allowed. Thus, the money was coined.

"Rocky, Yash, and I will take Hiccup and go to the market tomorrow to get supplies. Before we leave, is there any request." Oakra said, "Hang on, let's make a list. Ok."

They left the next morning with a short and simple list of supplies.

After an hour of walking, they finally reached the market. The market was busy with people. There were wooden stands everywhere like, in medieval times. The people were too scared to look up in fear that they might look a guard or troop in the eyes. There were stands no more than three feet from each other. Some of the shops had old fruit on the verge of spoiling. The butches had meat tied up across the front of their stands. There were a few shops, but the power didn't work very well, the lights flickered on and off, and the windows were broken.

"Ok, we need clothes, milk, eggs, ham, vegetables, and meat scraps. That is all of it, ok." Yash read off the list.

They had picked up everything on the list aside from meat scraps. They had started to ask around to see if anyone had meat scraps.

"NO, I don't have scraps for no mere mixed-up mutts! Now get lost!" a Market Butcher yelled.

"Wait, we will pay for the scraps. We only need a little bit. What are you going to use it in any way? If you don't want to sell the scraps to us, we can take our money elsewhere." Oakra replied, "Along with the rest of the meat we were going to buy. Have a good day, sir."

"Wait, what kind of scraps do you want, miss?" the butcher asked, waving his hands as they started to walk away.

"Any will do sir. Thank you," Yash responded.

The butcher handed them some scraps and meat. After that, they got a little wooden car for Luke and some rope for the dogs to play with.

"Hey, you guys, we are back." Yash hollered. Right then, red plowed over Rocky.

"What took you guys so long aside from a far walk? Are there more patrols out now? If so, we need to keep moving." Ace asked.

"No, we just had to get scraps and meat from a butcher in the market. That was all. There were no chicken eggs, and the only person that sells them was sick today." Rocky answered.

"So, no eggs?" Blaze asked.

"Not exactly," Yash replied.

"What do you mean?" Ace asked, confused.

"We got geese eggs instead," Rocky said.

"Luke, come here, we got you something to play with," Oakra said, handing him a wooden car.

"Hey, I will show you how to make paint so you can paint it if you would like." Ace said.

"Sure, thank you," Luke responded with a smile.

About an hour later, Ace and Oakra started dinner while Rocky, Luke, and Yash gathered wood for the fire later. Blaze took hiccup and Red on patrol one more time before a snowstorm moved in. They had all agreed to stay at the farmhouse until the snowstorm had passed. They figured they could gather people willing to fight for their cause and avoid getting caught in a snowstorm.

"Ok, pair up and pick rooms for the night," Oakra said.

It was barely even sunrise yet, and the farmhouse was silent when someone was banging on the door with some barking orders at some people. Luke pried out the window and covered his mouth because of Commander Cobie with some of his troops.

"Oakra, wake up. The troops are here. Get up." Luke whispered. "Wait, what? They are here. Ok, go wake up the others. I will handle the troops. Oh! Keep quiet." Oakra whispered as she rushed downstairs to answer the door.

"Yes, sir, may I help you? Are you looking for someone? Did you lose a search dog? If so, I saw a German Shepard that had GR states tags on in a small town that is not too far from here. I saw it about a day ago. Oh! My God, is there a criminal in this area? If so, I hope you catch them. Oh dear, where are my manners? Do you guys want something to drink or something to eat? You all must be starving? Can I help you with anything, though? Would you like to speak with my brother, sir? I hope you don't mind, but we were asleep. Sorry, it took so long to answer you." Oakra said, thinking quickly without looking them in the eyes.

"No need to worry, miss. We are just looking for the market nearby to pick up supplies. Thank you for the help, and I will keep an eye out for that dog." Commander Cobie said.

"Hello, Commander. I am sorry my sister tends to ask many questions at times. What are you and your soldiers looking for?" Rocky asked.

"Directions to the Market. Was the dog in the market as well?" Commander Cobie asked, looking at Oakra.

"Yes," Rocky answered quickly. After he knew that they were gone, he shut the door.

"What was that? They were about to leave!" Oakra yelled madder than ever.

"Well, you were asking too many questions. What else was I supposed to do! Either way, we have to leave now, so everyone needs to be ready to leave now. So, pack up." Rocky said.

"One, I had that. Two let me talk because they were getting ready to leave. Finally, I was acting like a local. What local would not freak out over a possible criminal in the area? If I did not act like a local, they would have thought we were hiding something, and if that was the case, we might as well come right out and say we are the rebellion. Third, I'm in charge." Oakra replied, "But you are right. It's time for us to leave before they come back."

They quickly began to pack as fast as possible. They made sure to grab weapons, food, and money. They each took a change of clothes and a spare pair of shoes.

"We can move faster through the woods." Ace said.

Very rarely did they take the roads. It took them 30 minutes to pack and be gone from the farmhouse for good.

Chapter Fifteen

Life or Death

"Is it safe to stop now? We have been traveling for seven hours now.

Come on; we're ten miles from the town and at least 25 miles from the farmhouse. At least for a drink or something. Come on, Rocky and Oakra, I'm exhausted. Can we please stop?" Luke asked.

"For the hundredth time, no! Not yet! It has been the same answer every time!" Rocky snapped.

"Soon, we passed some animal tracks that were wet, so that means there is water nearby." Oakra answered, turning to Rocky, "There was no need to snap at Luke like that! He is not used to being on the run like we are. Plus, Luke is a kid. So, was that truly needed?"

"Rocky, for your sake, don't answer that. Trust me; you already have a deep enough hole dug from this morning." Ace warned.

It was about 30 minutes later they found a small pond. The dock had vines growing up on the sides. There were lily pads and chickweed along the edge of the pond, and the water was murky. They could see fish and turtles bob their heads on the water to catch the bugs that landed. The smell of cucumbers was everywhere, and most of the ground was mush. Right then, Yash grabbed Ace's arm to pull her back and pointed to the ground. On the ground, in front of them was a rather large snake coiled up ready to strike. It was a copperhead.

"Someone needs to get up here and kill this snake before it bites one of us. Now would be nice." Yash whispered.

"Hang on, you two. Whatever you do, don't move." Rocky said, coming up behind the snake.

The second the snake turned around to strike, Rocky cut its head off. You were able to see the snake's jaw split in half. Then Rocky turned to see if Ace and Yash were ok. With a nod of their head, he walked off to check for any other snakes.

"Oakra, come over here." Rocky hollered.

"Now, what is it?" Oakra asked.

"We are not camping here tonight. There is too much of a chance of someone getting bit by a snake." Rocky replied, pointing to larger snakeskin and freshly hatched snake eggs on the side of the pond.

"Hey, you guys over here, I found a message from some of the rebellion, and it is fresh." Blaze said, waving them over to her.

"We are not far behind them, about a day or so behind them," Rocky replied.

"We will meet up with the rest of the rebellion," Oakra said.

Before they left, Ace had left a message for any other rebellion groups that came through that area. They had walked about six miles before the sun started to set. Rocky went on guard when he heard a wolf howl in the woods nearby where they were setting up the camp.

The second Oakra heard. She sprang up, almost falling out of the tree that she had forgotten that she was in. There, about 40 yards away, a white wolf stood on a rock howling at the moon, as its feet sat an almost solid black pup.

"Rocky, come up here, look how close they are?" Oakra asked.

"Yes, they are a little close for comfort," Rocky replied, uneasy about the wolf pack being so close.

"Hey, do you two see the wolves? I can hear them, and they are close, but I can't tell how close they are to us." Yash asked, looking around.

"They are about 40 yards away from camp." Oakra answered, "Get a fire going ASAP. Dig a tunnel underneath it to redirect the smoke. That will help keep away the wolves, but we are perfectly safe where we are at."

BANG! Someone had fired off a gun. Then they heard yipping, growling, and howling from some of the wolves.

"What was that?" Luke asked.

"Someone shooting wolves. For some reason." Blaze answered, looking around.

About ten minutes had passed, and there were at least eleven gunshots.

"Either someone got stuck in the middle of the pack, or they are poaching," Oakra replied, jumping out of the tree, "Rocky and Ace, you two stay with Luke and Red. Yash and Blaze, you two are with me and Hiccup. We are going to check out what is going on. Blaze your bobcat should stay here with the others, so they have a lookout."

When they got to where the wolf pack was, they saw dead wolves everywhere. Some were missing their hides, while others were missing their body parts. Then they noticed that a few of them had pups who were missing.

"Well, I guess that answers our question. It was poachers. It is such a shame that this is what people would do for money. Come on, let's get out of here before they come back for the white one." Oakra said while walking back to camp.

"Oakra, wait for a minute, look there is a small pup under the rock. They must have missed it. Let's take it back with us." Yash replied, picking up the wolf pup.

"Ok, but hurry up," Oakra responded, looking around for the poachers.

Once they got back to camp, they decided to leave at sunrise. The next day they packed everything and left. The rebellion had followed a small spring-fed creek. There was still no sign of the other rebellion members that had crossed through here the day before. Right then, a spear came flying past Luke and Rocky's heads.

"State your business, trespassers!" a shadow yelled from the treetops.

Then another spear rocketed past their heads. "He asked you a question," a female voice said.

"Answer them," Luke said, looking at Yash.

"Are you guys' nuts?!" Yash yelled.

"We are looking for the people who left a hidden message at the pond." Oakra said with a smile, "Now you answer my questions. Who are you? Are you the ones that left that message?"

"You do not have to answer that. We are just passing through," Rocky responded quickly.

"Yes, they do. We answered theirs. Now they are going to answer our question." Oakra said, looking at the treetops, "We are not leaving until we get an answer."

"Oakra, stop being so stubborn. Let's go before we get killed." Rocky said, pulling at her arm.

"It is too bad we are not answering." the male shadow said.

Right then, Oakra pulled out her bow and fired an arrow. The arrow had barely missed the shadow's head.

"Now answer, or I am climbing up that tree and knocking you out myself!" Oakra yelled irately.

"Let's just leave Oakra," Rocky said.

"Wait, did you say Oakra? That means you are Rocky, and you guys are one of the rebel groups. Right?" the girl asked.

"Depends on who's asking." Blaze replied, waiting for one of them to answer her.

"We are not telling you until you answer our question. Tick tock. We are waiting." the shadows said.

Chapter Sixteen

Friend or Foe

"So, are you Oakra?" the girl asked.

"I will answer you, but then you have to tell us who you guys are. Do we have a deal?" Oakra responded.

"Yes, we have a deal." the girl replied.

"Yes, my name is Oakra. Now it's your turn." Oakra said.

"We are some of Ziggy's troops." the girl answered.

"If that is true, then finish this. The wolves' howls hide our sound. Creeks are to show us the way and hide our scent. What is the rest of it?" Oakra said, stirring in the trees, waiting for an answer.

"The woods are to hide us, and the animals are to protect us." they both said.

"Good. We are here over the message you left at the pond." Oakra said.

"See, this is why we ask before we fire!" another voice yelled from another tree behind them.

"Ok, follow us." the girl said, jumping out of the treetop.

Their camp was hidden by bamboo and weeping willow trees. The ground around it was almost a swamp because of how much water there was.

"Oakra! It is so nice to see you again." Ziggy said, pleased to see Oakra.

"Long time no see," Oakra replied.

"Well, I thought you were eaten by wolves or coyotes." a woman from the past said, glaring at Oakra.

"Well, then you thought wrong, Mrs. Queens," Oakra said.

Ziggy and Oakra had gone to the academy that Mrs. Queens ran for the War States. Oakra and Ziggy had escaped the school by climbing over the fence using the oak tree. Ziggy was 5'2" with an average build. Her hair was short and brown, her eyes were blue, wearing a belly shirt and torn-up jeans. Mrs. Queens was 5'6" with a slim build. Her hair was black and in a tight librarian's bun. Her eyes were blue, and she had thin black glasses and was still wearing the uniform she wore at the academy.

"Ziggy, can I talk to you?" Oakra asked, staring at Mrs. Queens.

"Sure thing," Ziggy answered.

"Not trying to question you at all, but what is she doing here? In case you forgot, she was working for the War States." Oakra replied with concern.

"I know but we have guards keeping a close eye on her." Ziggy replied.

After showing them the camp and where their quarters are. They went to eat. They had hog and coon for dinner, with peas and corn to accompany it. There were about ten people, not counting Ziggy and Mrs. Queens. The following day Mrs. Queens went out to get blueberries for breakfast. The only thing is she was not grabbing blueberries; instead, she was picking poison berries and forever sleeping mushrooms. Then she went down to the market to get arsenic to make sure to kill some of the rebellion. By the time she got back, it was high noon. It was too late for her to make breakfast, but not too late for lunch or even a snack. She went into the tent for the kitchen and started cooking soup for the rebellion. She put coon and hog meat in it then tossed it with peas and corn.

She then mashed up the berries and mushrooms and mixed them with water before pouring them into the soup.

"Don't forget, Mrs. Queens, you are cooking dinner tonight," Ziggy said.

"Oh yes, I am working on a surprise for dinner now." Mrs. Queens

said, stirring the soup.

"Ok, thanks," Ziggy said, walking out of the tent.

Right then, Oakra jumped out of the tree, landing in front of Ziggy.

"Oakra, you scared me. What is the matter? That look you have means you believe something is wrong." Ziggy said, looking back at the tent.

"Yes, I believe she is up to something. I just don't know what yet." Oakra said, then Oakra went in the tent with Mrs. Queens, "I know you are up to something."

"Ziggy wants to talk to you," Rocky informed, walking out of the tent with Oakra.

"The troops are back from their run. Would you like to meet them?" Ziggy asked, waving them over to her. As the troops came over, Ace joined the rest of the tribe. The tribe is the part of the rebellion that Oakra runs.

"You guys already met Gem and Brick. These are Roset, Jove, Jet, Pepper, Winter, Jack, Rio, and Pan." Ziggy said.

Gem was 5'5" with a curvy build. Her eyes were green, and her hair was dark brown.

Brick had black hair and blue eyes. He was 5'8" and had a muscular build.

Roset had short blond hair and brown eyes. She was 5'1" and had a slim build.

Jove had long brown hair and gray eyes. She was 5'3" with a medium build.

Jet had short blond hair, green eyes, was 5'6", with a small build.

Pepper had black hair with white highlights, and her eyes were brown. She was 5'4" and had a slim build.

Winter had snow-white hair, blue eyes, 5'3", and she had a curvy build.

Jack had brown hair and brown eyes, and he was leaning against a log by the fire.

Rio was sitting under a tree. His hair was black, and his eyes were emerald, green.

Pan had dirty blond hair and brown eyes. He was 5'6" tall and had a strong build.

"Well, I guess that just leaves the tribe," Oakra said.

"This is Rocky, Yash, Luke, Ace, and Blaze. I'm Oakra. It is very nice to meet you." Oakra introduced them to the others.

"Sorry to interrupt, but dinner is ready." Mrs. Queens said.

They all sat around the fire pit to eat. The soup was very runny and brown with a touch of purple. The smell was a mixture of coon and pine.

"I added some pine tea to the soup for some more flavor." Mrs. Queens answered as Oakra looked at the soup, debating whether to eat it.

Mrs. Queens used pine tea to cover the smell of rotten cow meat. "Aren't you going to eat with us, Mrs. Queens?" Oakra questioned, meeting Ms. Queens with a gaze.

"Yeah, at least come for a cup of tea or famous soup. We don't bite." Ziggy said, figuring out what Oakra was up to.

"No thanks, I already ate tonight. You guys go ahead and eat." Mrs. Queens replied swiftly.

"Come on. Come at least one bite of soup." Oakra insisted. "She doesn't have to," Luke said.

"It tastes great. Mrs. Queens." Rio said with his bowl almost gone. "Thank you, but I really must be getting to bed." Mrs. Queens replied, walking around, "It has been a long day. Don't let the tea go to waste, please."

After that, Ziggy went to her tent without eating. Luke sat and finished his bowl, and Rio went back to seconds.

"Rocky and Yash, tomorrow I will need you two to make a run to the market for medical supplies we are running low. I will make a list for you two. I have a hunch that we are going to need it." Oakra informed them, then walked over toward Ziggy.

"Oakra, who all ate the soup? We need to be sure we have plenty of meds for them. Plus, we need to know how much they ate." Ziggy asked worriedly.

"Rio had two bowls, Luke had one and Winter had about a quarter of her bowl. No one has drunk the tea yet. Rocky and Yash are going to town to get the meds tomorrow morning." Oakra answered, turning her head to the fire pit.

They went into the cooking tent to see what kind of medical supplies would be needed. That is when they found traces of arsenic.

"What is that smell?" Ziggy asked, covering her nose.

Before Oakra had a chance to look around, she stepped in a pile of rotting meat. The smell was about seven days old. Then they found the remains of the poison berries.

Later that night, they had a rude awakening. Rio was burning up and not waking up. Luke, and Winter were burning up but still awake. Brick raced down to the stream to get some water for them.

"Rocky and Yash, make that trip tonight. Here is the list. Now go! Ace gets some covers. Blaze towels and rags. Gem, you need to heat some water ASAP." Oakra Ordered.

"Pan, Jack, and Roset find Mrs. Queens and bring her to us. By force, if need be. Wait, where is Jove?" Ziggy demanded, looking around.

"She was not feeling well after she drank the tea, so she went to bed." Jet answered, staring at Oakra and Ziggy, trying not to panic.

"Jet, go get Jove and bring her here. Pepper, try to wake Rio." Oakra ordered once more.

After that, Oakra walked over to the animals to make sure that Mrs. Queens didn't poison them.

"What could have caused this?" Blaze asked, puzzled.

"Mrs. Queens tried to poison everyone," Oakra replied, looking at the others.

Right then, Jack, Pan, and Roset came back without Mrs. Queens. "She is long gone," Pan said.

"Ok, then we will beef up patrol around the camp," Ziggy responded. Right then, Rocky and Yash came back with the medical supplies.

They quickly pulled out the meds and started to pass them around to the ones that were sick.

"They are here. Get ready." Gem warned.

"There are four troops plus Mrs. Queens." Jet informed.

"Is General Einstein one of them?" Ziggy asked.

"Yes," Jet answered.

"I got this. Just keep quiet. Hiccup, come." Oakra said.

Oakra went to meet the troops at the edge of the woods. She turned on her flashlight and slowly walked up to the troops to stop them in their tracks.

"There you are. We have been looking everywhere for you prisoner." Oakra lied, grabbing Mrs. Queen's arm, "Thought you would get away with killing an officer, did you?"

"Wait, what are you talking about?" General Einstein asked.

"She is a patient at the trauma psych ward. While she was escaping, she had stabbed an officer to death. I have been looking for her to take back to the psych ward. You see, she is a danger to others. She sees things that are not there." Oakra explained, "I have been tracking her for the past ten towns. Hoping she has not harmed anyone else."

"Very well, can we put her in a clinic here to save you the trouble of taking her back by yourself?" General Einstein asked, "Have you seen anyone else here?"

"Yes, you may; thank you so much. I will let the trauma psych ward know that she is in your clinic here. I have not seen a single soul since the last town." Oakra replied, watching the troops walk away with Mrs. Queens kicking and screaming.

Chapter Seventeen

This Means War

It was five days after they had been poisoned. Luke and Winter's fever had gone down, and they were almost back to their old selves. Rio was still running a fever and would not eat anything but was doing much better than the first night. Some of the rebellion was still shaken up by what had happened.

"This is the most I have seen them moving in almost a week," Rocky said, watching them walk around camp.

"I know." Jet replied.

"Hey, Oakra, what did you do with Mrs. Queens?" Gem asked.

"Well, I had convinced the troops that she was nuts and killed an officer when she escaped the psych ward," Oakra responded, walking past them.

It was mid-day when Ace and Blaze came back with a hog for dinner. While Rocky was cleaning the hog, Yash, and Jet went to the market.

"Ok, we need; fruit, blankets, medical supplies, rags, boots, and metal." Jet said, reading off the list.

"Ok, what is bolded?" Yash asked.

"Fruit, medical supplies, and boots." Jet replied.

"Ok, then that is our top priority. We will get those first." Yash responded.

When they got back, it was almost dark, and some of them had already fallen asleep.

"Kill it! Shut it! Someone kill it! I don't care who kills it. Someone just kill it!" Winter was screaming, standing on a stump, pointing at a skunk.

"Winter, stop yelling and back up slowly," Oakra ordered, waving slowly to her.

The skunk was getting ready to spray Winter. Oakra had gotten Winter's attention, but it was too late. The skunk had sprayed her.

"Gem, take her to the creek. Jet, go get her tomato soup, and Blaze, can you go get her a towel and a fresh change of clothes." Ziggy said, watching the skunk run out of camp.

Three days later, the smell was almost gone, and they began to pack up the camp to keep moving. Lucky Ziggy had a van so they could take the roads for a little bit. After two days on the road, they sold the van and went on foot through the woods to avoid the War States' troops.

"Hey, there is more of the rebellion somewhere through this area. Maybe we can stop soon for a short break." Ziggy said.

"Maybe, but it is if we keep going. There are fresh tracks and nice green vegetation, so there should be a source of water nearby." Oakra suggested, "Plus, we need to cover more ground before we stop to set up camp."

Out of nowhere, Hiccup went haywire. When they turned around, there was a large female grizzly bear following behind them. What they did not see was two cubs playing in trees right above them.

As they began to back up, she stood up on her hind legs and growled, then went back on all fours. Then she started to walk toward them.

"Everyone slowly back up and make every little noise," Oakra said, grabbing Luke's arm to pull him back a little.

As Rocky stepped back, a tree branch fell and almost hit him.

"Look up, Oakra, what is in the trees above us?" Rocky asked, looking at the branch behind him.

"It is two cubs. Just back up slowly and do not walk to the grove of trees. Once we are away from her cubs, we will be safe. No one raises any weapons or any that appear like one." Oakra explained, backing up away from the trees.

After that, they kept walking for seven miles to make sure they were out of the bears' territory. They were not able to find a creek, river, pond, or lake, but they found an old barn that was missing some boards and a shallow well that was not dried up yet.

"This reminds me of when storms would hit before everything happened. When we would sit and tell ghost stories." Ziggy said, looking at the barn.

"Ok. The fire is going now." Yash informed, putting some deadwood in the fire to make it hotter.

They did this because if the temperature was hot enough, there would be no smoke. If there was no smoke, they took less chance of running into the troops or guards.

Later that night, Ziggy woke up with a rattlesnake by her hand.

"Jove, wake up." Ziggy whispered, "Jove, please wake up."

"What, Ziggy? Holy cow!!! There is a rattlesnake in here!" Jove yelled.

"I know. Just kill it already." Ziggy whispered.

Jove pulled her sword from its sheath and sent the sword tip into the snake's head-splitting it in half. After they both calmed down, they fell back to sleep. About an hour after, they all woke up and started to make breakfast.

"We have three hours to eat and pack up," Oakra said, packing up some of the supplies.

"Why?" Jove asked, puzzled.

"Because this area is crawling with troops, and there is no safe way through or around town if we wait any longer. If we take too long, we will chance traveling these paths at night, and that is not safe either." Oakra explained.

"There is no safe way around the town. So, what are we going to do?" Yash replied, looking at the map.

"I know. That is why we are going through the town. I will be back." Oakra said.

An hour later, Oakra came back with a van. They traveled on the road for five days, then sold the van and went on foot once more. The woods that they were tracking through seemed too quiet. Every now and then they could hear voices when they would stop. They were beginning to believe that someone was following them.

"How much longer?" Luke asked.

"About two to three days," Ziggy answered.

"That is if they did not move again. Like they did last time." Rocky remarked.

"Have some hope, Rocky," Jove responded with a smile.

"Jove is right. If we keep moving at this rate, we should be able to catch up to them before they leave." Oakra replied.

"Can we set up camp now?" Rio asked. "Here soon. Right?" Pepper said.

"Yes, it is too dark to keep traveling. We will set up camp here for the night." Oakra answered.

"Who has the first watch tonight?" Brick asked.

"I can take the first watch," Jove said.

Later that night, Jove thought she saw someone, but the figure was gone before she could get a second look. The next day at high noon, Yash saw some writing on a tree.

"Hey, here is a message. It's on this old oak tree." Yash said. "You're close by high noon; you should find us in the cover of the dark." Ace read.

It was about four hours later when Jove saw the person again. Right then, a bullet came flying past Ziggy's head.

"Everyone, take cover!" Oakra yelled, waving at the trees. Thud!

"Stay low and hit the trees," Jove exclaimed, as she knocked Pepper to the ground.

As Jove started to get up, a bullet hit her in the chest.

"Jove!!!" Pepper screamed as a guard grabbed her, "Let me go! Put me down now! Someone help!!"

"Pepper, Jove!!! Let them go!!!!" Jack yelled, coming out from behind the trees.

As soon as Jack stepped out of the tree line, the War State troops started to shoot. The second they started to fire, Jack hit the ground, and a bullet caught him on the side of the head. After they had shot Jack, they left with Jove and Pepper.

"Jack, get up! Come on, Jack. You got to wake up! Please, Jack!" Winter yelled, putting pressure on the gunshot wound while holding back her tears.

"Luke, go get a sheet from the bag. Rocky, Yash, and Brick go, get some branches. Ace clean rags. Ziggy bandages and gauzes. Blaze alcohol so we can clean the wound out. Winter keep pressure on the wound." Oakra ordered.

Once they got the wound treated and the stretcher was made, they got the animals and left.

"Ok, we are going to split into two groups. Group one will come with me to get Jove and Pepper, and group two will keep going till you find somewhere safe and keep an eye on Jack. Once we get them, group one will meet up with you guys when we know that we are not being followed." Oakra said, grabbing her weapons.

"Luke, Ace, Winter, and Brick will stay with Jack. The smaller the group, you have the better." Rocky ordered, "Yash, Blaze, Ziggy, Oakra, and I are group one. We will also be taking Hiccup. The other animals will stay with group two. Now move out."

After about two hours tracking the troops, they had finally found their base. The base looked like it was an old military base. There were four gray metal buildings on the property. A ten-feet electric fence went all the way around the base. Then there was an outer fence made of barbed wire that was four-feet tall. The only visible way in was the front gate for the military vehicles. Outside there were fifteen guards and ten troops.

"What are we going to do? There are guards everywhere." Ziggy asked.

"We are going to use an EMP arrow to shut down the power and security systems for a few minutes. Then all that leaves us to do is get past the guards without being noticed. We only use force if needed. We do not need to be seen." Oakra explained.

"But you only have a few EMP arrows left." Ziggy pointed out. "This is what they were made for. So make it count." Oakra replied.

They had got in without being seen but did not have too long before the EMP arrow's effects wore off. When they found the building and the floor where the others were being held, they started to make their way down to the last floor, which was three stories under the ground level. The floor where Pepper and Jove were being held looked like a prison. The cells were six by six with a bed and toilet in each one. There were about forty cells on this floor.

"Pepper, are you here?" Blaze asked.

"Over here, hurry up, before the guard comes back," Pepper whispered.

As they were helping Pepper out of her cell, they noticed that Jove was not with her.

"Where is Jove?" Yash asked.

"She…. she… She is dead. They shot her in the chest. I tried to stop the bleeding but could not even slow it down. After she died, they took her body. They said they needed one of her kidneys. They have not come back since then." Pepper explained, sobbing.

"It is ok you did your best," Ziggy replied, placing her hand on Pepper's shoulder.

"Hang on, are you sure she is dead?" Yash asked. "Yes," Pepper replied, still crying.

"Ok, then it is time for us to get out of here before we are discovered," Oakra responded, checking to see if it was safe to move yet.

When they had got back, Jack was still out cold from the gunshot, but the bleeding had stopped.

"Is he going to be, ok?" Pepper asked, holding her hands over her mouth in shock.

"He will be fine. We are just waiting on him to wake up." Ace answered, looking up at Pepper.

After Pepper sat down by Jack, the others began to debate what their next move should be.

"Where is Jove? Is… Is she dead?" Luke struggled to ask them. "Yes. She did not make it. We are sorry to be the bearers of bad news." Ziggy answered, dropping her head and looking at the ground, "We can't let her die in vain."

"I am with Ziggy on this one. What is our next move?" Ace asked.

"We fight back. No more running. My suggestion is to join up with the other groups, hit them hard, and take them out." Rocky replied.

"No. Not yet, the War States know that we are here. and they will see that coming from a mile away. We need to have a plan to attack them." Oakra argued, trying to be a voice of reason.

"We need to act now!" Rocky yelled.

"How in the world do you think that is going to work? We have people injured, so we have smaller numbers. Are we going to charge in with no plan, and as blind as a bat, we will surely be shot down left and right. That will not help anyone. Will it? We scout their bases for the weakest points. Then we take out the heads of command. After that, we regroup with the rest of the rebellion and go after the leaders. They would expect us to let our anger cloud our judgment." Oakra argued, angrily staring Rocky down.

"So, what if your plan fails, then what?" Rocky asked with a cocky tone.

"Then we will use force, but nobody that is not involved is to be harmed. If it comes to that, we need to make sure that there are no civilians in the crossfire understood and we have the numbers," Oakra stated, "The next group is the flags. Odysseus is in charge of this group."

"Fine. We will do this your way. How many more groups do we have to meet up with?" Rocky said.

"Three more because most of the groups already met up and are waiting at D.C for us. We must be careful because we are at one of the largest points in the War States. It is one of the three capitals we are approaching." Oakra explained.

"Plus, we don't have a full proof-plan." Blaze stated.

Chapter Eighteen

Regroup

"State your reason for entering these grounds, civilians." Nightshade said.

He did not look any different from the last time they met. This time he was wearing blue camo.

"We are here to meet up with the flag for transport," Oakra replied. "Western fighters???" Nightshade asked.

"Yes," Rocky replied.

"Good. It is Nightshade. It's been a while since I saw you guys?" Nightshade stated.

"I know it has been," Oakra answered. "It is time to regroup now," Rocky said.

"I see. Follow me." Nightshade said, waving them to come.

Later that night, they met up with Odysseus, the leader of the flags.

"I was beginning to think that you guys had been killed off like the Patriots that were in the badlands," Odysseus said.

"Well, there goes that strength in numbers that you were hoping for Oakra, the Patriots were one of the largest groups in the rebellion." Rocky Said.

"So, what do you guys' plan if you were hoping for strength in numbers?" Odysseus asked.

"We will regroup and fight back," Oakra said.

"How? We are way outnumbered now. Most of the larger groups were killed or captured because they didn't separate like they were supposed to. We have a slim chance of beating the war states. All three of the rulers are ruthless." Nightshade asked, shocked that there was no proper plan yet.

"We will figure the rest out when we regroup with the rest of the rebellion. For now, let's eat." Rocky replied.

"I agree. Let's eat." Odysseus said, nodding in agreement.

The flags had simple hard-to-spot traps around for protection. There was barbed wire that was ankle height, bear traps, and a few snares.

"So, where do we go from here?" Nightshade asked.

"To look for more fighters though the Appalachian Mountains and the east coast." Yash replied looking up from the fire.

"How are we going to get past the war states?" Odysseus asked. "Leave that one to me," Oakra responded, standing up and walking away.

After that, they all went to bed as it started to pour down. The next

morning, they packed up and made their way through the muddy, swampy land caused by the rainstorm the night before.

"Odysseus, I am hot and hungry." a little girl said with black hair and blue eyes.

She was about ten years of age. Her name was Katherian.

"I know, but we can't do anything until we find water and a place to set up camp," Odysseus replied.

"Ok," Katherian responded, continuing to walk once more.

"Hey, look there is some water!" Julius exclaimed, running towards the water.

THUD!!!

"Sssssshhhhh," Katherian said with her finger over her lips after tackling Julius to the ground.

"What was that for?" Julius whispered.

"Look, a bounty hunter," Katherian replied, pointing at a man with her hand trembling in fear.

The man was about six foot eight and had on dark blue jeans, a leather jacket, and combat boots. His hair was dark brown; they were unable to see his eyes past his jet-black sunglasses. Right then, the bounty hunter collapsed and rolled down a small hill stopping just before he hit the water.

"What in the world was that?!" Julius exclaimed in shock while scrambling to his feet and covering Katherian's head.

"We need to take cover behind those rocks," Katherian said, pointing at some large rocks.

Oakra, Rocky, Yash, and Jack were already hiding behind the rocks. "What was that?" Rocky asked.

"I don't know," Katherian responded, looking around for an explanation.

"Hold up. There is a dart in the bounty hunter's neck." Jack pointed out, looking through his binoculars.

"Cover me. Watch the trees and the edge of those buffs." Oakra replied, using the trees as cover to go to check on the bounty hunter to see if he was alive.

Oakra slowly crept over to him with her bow ready to fire at a split second. She kneeled to the ground, placing her bow on the ground to check his pulse. She pulled the dart out of his neck to see what kind of dart hit him. The dart was painted red and yellow with turkey feathers on the back. It was hollowed out in the center for some kind of poison or tranquilizer.

She checked his pulse, but he was dead. She slowly turned around, picking up her bow drawing an arrow ready to fire if needed. She kept low and used the trees and bushes for the cover.

"So, what was it? Who was it?" Julius asked.

"Oakra fire off a signal arrow," Rocky said.

"Not a good idea. If they are not friendly and see if they will figure out who we are. They will not be able to see it as well in the daylight. We use the sound signal. Jack, you're up." Oakra commented, nodding her head, "Wait before you shot. It might be a friend."

Jack made a sound similar to a screech owl.

"So, what does that do?" Luke asked.

"It lets other rebellion members know we are friendlies," Jack answered.

"Each sector has three signals. One is marking the trees with messages, the second one is the arrows which create a colored explosion of glass and fire, and the third one is sound. We use mimicry of certain animals. Each group has their own animals to copy." Katherian explained.

"Ok, so now what?" Luke asked.

"We wait. It might be more rebellion members." Jack answered.

Right then, a sound of a coyote in distress responded.

"Wait! Was that a distress signal? Jack one more time. I want to find out if that is a distress signal or just a coyote." Oakra ordered.

Jack signaled once more, but they received the same response.

 "Ok. Then Katherian, Luke, Jack, and Julius go back to the others, stay low and send Ace, Blaze, Odysseus, and Nightshade. Tell them to bring weapons. We don't know what we are walking into. Make it fast and stay in the trees and brush because it will be harder for anyone to shoot you." Oakra ordered, looking for an easy way up to the bluffs without being seen.

"What are you looking at?" Rocky asked.

"Away up, but there is not a safe way up. We will have to go around. Yash, look on your map and find us the fastest way up with the most cover." Oakra responded.

Yash pulled out an old rolled-up map that was about four-feet wide and five-feet long and covered in dust.

"Do I want to know where this map came from?" Rocky asked, looking at a label saying property of the GR States.

"An old War States bunker. It looked like it hadn't been used in years. Where else would I get a map like this?" Yash answered, looking up from the map.

"Are you stupid or something? Do you realize what will happen if you get caught with this?" Rocky asked angrily.

"I am fully aware, but we need a map, and they were not using it. So, I don't see the harm. Now shut the hell up so I can find a way around the bluffs." Yash responded.

"Excuse the hell out of me. You do not tell me to shut up. Keeping that map is not safe and an extremely bad idea." Rocky yelled.

"I say we need the map, because without it, we will be going in blind and would already be dead. So, get off my case." Yash responded, standing up.

"Knock it off both of you two. If you keep yelling at each other, we will be caught. So, stop playing who the alpha male or I am going to beat the living hell out of you both. The map is a 50 50 shot, either way, so we keep it." Oakra said, putting herself in between them to prevent a fight.

"Damn, what on earth are you two fighting over? We could hear you all the way from there." Odysseus pointed out.

"So, what is the plan, Oakra?" Blaze asked.

"Well, I will let you know that when Yash finds us a way past those bluffs because going straight up is not an option. We will be seen taking that way, and it is too steep." Oakra replied, glaring at both Rocky and Yash.

"Wait! What if it is a trap?" Ace asked with a concerned look.

"It is a possibility, but we will not know until we get there. So, we need to be careful." Oakra replied, "Any luck?"

"Yeah. If we cut them down a little way, we can use this cedar, thick it as cover. It's not as quick as you'd want, but it's the only way to provide us enough cover to avoid being shot. So, I hope that is ok." Yash answered, rolling the map back up.

"Yes, that is ok. Move out." Oakra replied.

They were walking for an hour through the mud and thorn bushes when Rocky heard a rattle. He had stepped on the midsection of a six-foot timber rattlesnake.

"Oh, shit!!!!!" Rocky yelled, pulling out his Glock 19 pistol.

Right as the snake launched itself toward Rocky ready to bite him, he fired the gun blowing the snake's head to bits.

"Great!! Just great. You better hope that whoever is at the top of the bluffs did not hear that. Why in the hell would you fire off that damn gun with how loud it is?" Yash yelled.

"Well, what else was I going to do?" Rocky asked furiously.

"No, but maybe use the hatchet on your damn site," Yash replied. "Oh and put my hand by the snake's mouth. No thanks." Rocky yelled, stepping toward Yash.

"Do these two get into fights like this often?" Odysseus asked. "Only when they disagree, which is all the time." Ace answered. Oakra bent down and pulled out her knife to cut off the rattle.

"That is enough from the both of you two. You both are too busy playing Alpha male smackdown to care that we are getting close to where the signal came from. We need to be focused on fighting the enemy, not each other so knock it the hell off before you get us caught. I don't know, nor do I care why? You two keep fighting, but it needs to stop. You guys are acting like children. Am I clear?" Oakra snapped at them while waving the rattle at them both.

"Who is there?" a rather tall soldier covered in scars that looked like they were from a fire.

"Wait, Oakra, isn't that the soldier you caught on fire two years ago?" Rocky asked, placing his arm in front of her backing her up toward the others.

"Find a place to hide Oakra, Ace, and Blaze," Yash replied. "Hey, over here, you guys," Nightshade whispered, waving from the small cave hidden by trees and grapevines.

They all hid in the small cave. When the soldier got close to the cave, Oakra started to shake the rattle from the timber rattler that Rocky had shot ten minutes earlier. The soldier quickly stepped away from the cave thinking it was a rattlesnake.

They stayed in a cave for maybe an hour to be sure that it was safe.

"I think that they would be gone by now," Odysseus said, stepping out of the cave unaware of the snipper watching the big open spot about 20 yards to the left of him.

"Odysseus, wait. It might be a trap. Odysseus, get back here." Oakra pleated, looking around.

"It is ok. See, I am fine." Odysseus replied, walking closer to the clearing that the snipper was watching.

"Odysseus, get back here. That's an order. It is not safe." Oakra demanded in hopes that Odysseus would listen to her.

"Look, Oakra, everything is fine. The guy is gone. He was probably gone 40 minutes ago." Odysseus replied, spinning in a circle to prove it was safe.

"I will go get him," Nightshade responded, pulling out a few pipe bombs from his bag.

At the very second Nightshade moved a vine to step out of the cave, a flash grenade went off, followed by smoke bombs. Then the soldiers grabbed Odysseus while he was unable to fight back and fled with him. They packed him about 3 miles from the cave before meeting up with Commander Cobie.

"Sir, we have a live one for you." a low-ranked soldier said. pushing Odysseus to the ground.

"Is this all of them?" Commander Cobie asked, grabbing Odysseus by the chin making him lookup.

"Ye... Yes... Sir." the soldier stumbled on his words.

"Are you sure that this is the last one in the area?" Commander Cobie asked, glaring at the lower-ranked soldier.

"Yes, we killed the ones at the top of the bluffs, and the bounty hunter was found dead. No doubt that it was the rebellion hiding out by the tops of those bluffs. Why do you ask, sir?" another soldier quickly answered.

"Because this is Odysseus! One of the leaders of the rebellion! Robert Smith's son! That is why!" Commander Cobie snapped at them.

"So, there are more here?" one of the soldiers asked.

"Yes. Take him back to base. Lets' see if we can't get him to squill like the filthy pig he is. Maybe the others are close by." Commander Cobie replied, with a brief pause, "Now!!!"

"Yes, sir" the low-ranked soldier responded, walking swiftly to the van. "What in the hell was that?" Nightshade asked.

"I don't know, but my ears are still ringing from it," Rocky replied. "It was a Flash grenade," Oakra answered, walking out of the cave. "Wait, where is Odysseus?" Ace asked looking, around.

"They used the flash grenade and smoke bombs to grab him, not knowing we were here," Rocky answered, picking up a smoke bomb.

"What makes you so sure?" Yash asked.

"If they knew we were here, they would have grabbed us too." Oakra answered, "Good thing you waited before you started to go get him, or they would have grabbed you and known we were here."

"Oakra, how could you say that" Nightshade asked.

"She is right. Think about it. If they caught us, how would we be able to save his dumb ass." Blaze pointed out.

"Come on, let's go back. We need to tell the others and figure out how to save him." Oakra replied, walking back to the others.

"Come on, we have a lot of ground and little sunlight left," Rocky said following Oakra.

There were about seven miles back to camp and two hours of daylight left.

Chapter Nineteen

To Tell or Not to Tell

"So, you are going by Odysseus now. From what I heard; you can tell me where some of the leaders are hiding. So, do we do this the easy way or the hard way? My dear sweet nephew." a man spoke from a dark corner of the room, holding a hammer.

"Well, isn't the backstabbing two-time double-crossing uncle William? What are you now, a lieutenant?" Odysseus remarked with a smile that said, drop dead.

"No, I am the interrogator. So, start talking." Officer Williams answered, slamming the hammer against Odysseus's hand.

With a slight smile, Odysseus stood up and spit in his uncle's face, and said, "I don't talk to traders. So go to hell."

"So, you chose the hard way. So be it." Officer William responded, pulling out a syringe and stabbing it in Odysseus's neck.

Within seconds he fell to the floor, fast asleep. "So, would he not talk?" Commander Cobie asked.

"I wish you would not have killed all of the others. They would have sung like birds. This one just has a loudmouth and will not talk." Officer William said.

"Well, he is your nephew, so offer him a deal. I want those leaders now. We kill them, and the rebellion falls. If we can't stop them, they will tear this government apart. So, he talks, or you will need a hole in the ground to join your brother. Now go." Commander Cobie ordered.

"Yes, sir," Officer William replied, starting to open the door.

"William, I mean it. He talks, or you join your brother in the ground." Commander Cobie said.

When Odysseus woke up, he was chained to a dark blue chair used for interrogation.

"Well, it looks like you are awake." Officer William said, dumping a bucket of frigidly cold water on him.

"When I get free, I am going to use these chains to choke you out. Then I am going to gouge out your eyes with my cuffs." Odysseus threatened, looking right at his uncle.

"Listen to me very closely, Oscar. I don't wish for them to kill you, so I talked to them, and they are willing to offer you a deal. I can give you your freedom if you join us and tell us where the other leaders are hiding. So do we have a deal?" Officer William explained, smiling.

"Ummmm. Let me think about it. Oh yes. No way in hell I am going to trust you or rat out my true family. I will not be like you." Odysseus replied, sitting back in the chair.

"So, you will side with people who are not blood? Come on, my dear sweet nephew, think about it. You will have respect and power if you help us. Come on; the clock is ticking." Officer William responded, placing his hand on Odysseus's shoulder.

"Drop dead. I wouldn't help you even if hell froze over." Odysseus remarked, still holding a smile.

"Fine, then have it your way." Officer William replied, pulling a pair of pliers out and began pulling off his fingernails. "Care to talk now?"

"Nope, I told you not even if hell froze over," Odysseus answered, still trying to smile.

After that, William started to break each one of Odysseus's knuckles.

"How about now? It will save a lot of time for me and a lot of pain for you." Officer William instated.

"Drop dead. I know even if I talk, I will be killed, so why bother? Why rat out my family? Like, I said, I am not like you." Odysseus replied.

No sooner than Odysseus finished his sentence, Officer William slammed the hammer from earlier onto his hand, listening to the rest of the bones break in his right hand.

"I swear, you are even more bullheaded than your old man, but by the time I am done with you I will have you squealing like a pig in the slaughterhouse." Officer William remarked, raising the hammer again.

Then he slammed the hammer onto Odysseus's left hand, shattering the bones in it.

"Look, wouldn't it just be easier to talk?" Officer William asked.

"Is that the best you got? If so, you are going to be a laughingstock. I can just imagine you losing your job because you could not get your own nephew to talk." Odysseus insulted, smiling.

"William, out here now!" Commander Cobie ordered.

"Yes, sir." Officer William responded, stepping outside and closing the door behind him.

"That is not working. Go, get the rat and cane. If that does not work, get the snake." Commander Cobie said.

"Sir, and if neither of these options work, then what?" Officer William asked.

"Just make your damn nephew talk. Dictator Charles is growing tired of waiting." Commander Cobie said, walking down the hallway.

"So, I see you got yelled at. Like I said, laughingstock." Odysseus said.

"Chain him to the table and make sure he doesn't move." Officer William ordered the guards, "Last chance to talk, Oscar."

"My name is not Oscar. It is Odysseus, and I told you to drop dead because I am not gonna talk a word." Odysseus snapped, pulling up, trying to fight back.

Once the guards had him chained to the table, Officer William walked up and ripped his shirt off. After that, he pulled a rat out of a wooden box and placed it on Odysseus's chest and placed a metal cane over it.

"Do you think a rat scares me?" Odysseus asked.

"No. it is not to scare you, but to make you talk." Officer William said, placing a blow touch to the cane.

Once the cane began to heat, the rat began to bite and claw at Odysseus's stomach. As Odysseus started to scream and yell in pain the more Officer William began to heat the can. After a minute of Odysseus screaming in pain, they stopped the can and lifted it.

"Care to talk now, my dear sweet nephew?" Officer William asked, smirking, thinking that Odysseus was getting ready to spill.

"What part of not even if hell froze over did you not understand?" Odysseus croaks with a small smile.

"Ok, then 30 more seconds." Officer William ordered.

The 30 seconds passed, but despite everything, Odysseus would not talk.

"Put him back in the chair and bring in the snake." Officer William said, looking right at his nephew.

"Oh! A snake so scary. Is that all you got?" Odysseus replied.

As they walked out, they locked the door to be sure Odysseus could not get free. Once the snake got close, Odysseus stood up and flopped down, causing the chair leg to land on the snake's head. There was blood everywhere.

"Now, what? Sir, nothing has worked, and I don't see anything working." Officer William stated.

"Starve him. He should talk to get food." Commander Cobie Said.

"Sir, I do not see it working. I broke all the bones in both hands and used the rat in a cane. I don't see starving him will make him talk." Officer William said.

"I don't care. Just make him talk, or you will join him." Commander Cobie said, looking in the room.

They waited three days before Officer William went back to the holding cell where Odysseus had kept.

"Are you hungry?" Officer William asked, holding a plate full of steak, corn, and rice.

"No, I am not," Odysseus answered.

"Fine, then are you thirsty?" Officer William asked.

"Trying to bribe me now. That is funny, but I am not talking. I will die before I do." Odysseus said.

"Why will you not just talk!?" Officer William yelled.

"This is how I view things. I talk to everyone I trust and call family members. If I don't, my family will be safe, Commander Cobie will kill you because I wouldn't talk, plus The War States will fall. So why should I talk." Odysseus said, smiling.

"That does it! I have tried everything to make you talk, but nothing has worked." Officer William snapped, pulling out his desert eagle, "Now stop wasting my damn time!!! Last warning, Oscar! Talk!!!!"

"Now, now. We both know that is an empty threat. You can't kill me because Commander Cobie thinks I will talk. Face it; you kill me he will kill you or hand you over to the chief. So, you don't scare me. I die, and I win. I live, I win because both ways I win, and you lose." Odysseus said, watching the door.

"Funny, but not true." Officer William said, placing his hand on the trigger.

"Are you sure?" Odysseus asked, smiling, still watching the door.

"Yes!" Officer William said, ready to pull the trigger.

"Then why does your boss seem so unhappy?" Odysseus said, smiling as Commander Cobie walked into the room.

"Com…Commander Co...Cobie I...I... I was not really going to sh...Shot him. I...I...I was just trying to scare it out of him. I...I...I promise s…sir" Officer William said with nothing but fear in his voice.

William knew that very second, he was in trouble. Without saying a word, Commander Cobie pulled out his Smith and Wesson revolver, cocked it, pointed it at Officer William's head and pulled the trigger.

BANG!!!!! Officer William's brain and blood painted the wall and covered Odysseus.

"Now, he may have been bluffing, but I am not. Start talking, or that will be you." Commander Cobie said, pointing the gun at Odysseus.

"Then kill me. I will not talk. The war states will fall. Then we will have our rights back. We will be free once more. So have fun wasting your time. Just remember the chief will be furious to find out you have been wasting time on me instead of searching for the leaders." Odysseus said, smirking.

"That does it stop stalling. If you don't talk, you will die slowly and painfully." Commander Cobie said as calmly as could be.

"I do not fear neither death nor you. The sad part is you were right about one thing. I am stalling, but not for me." Odysseus said, smiling, waiting for Commander Cobie to get the call.

Right then, he got a call from prison. A prison nearby had been blown up. They had escaped with Rocky, Blaze, and Yash before Ace blew it up.

"You are meaning to tell me you lost all of the prisoners!!!!!" Commander Cobie yelled into the phone then turned to Odysseus.

"I told you that you were wasting your time. Now have fun explaining how you wasted time letting the leaders get away with the prisoners. Not to Minchin, my backstabbing uncle William. I wonder if he is going to kill you, or will you lose your rank? I can't wait to see." Odysseus said laughing.

"Well, I guess you were right, you would die before you talk. Last chance, Oscar. You will make a fantastic soldier. Maybe even better than your uncle." Commander Cobie said, pointing the gun at Odysseus's head again.

"If I talk, you will shoot me, and if I don't even then, you will shoot me. So let me think. No, I will not die a trader like my backstabbing uncle. So go to hell, Commander Cobie. Go ahead, kill me, commander but remember one thing, this kingdom will fall, and the people will be free once more, and you will have died without horror." Odysseus said smiling.

"Fine, have it your way, Odysseus." Commander Cobie said, pulling the trigger.

Odysseus's body fell out of the chair. The walls were painted in Odysseus's blood, and the floor was covered in it. When Commander Cobie looked down at Odysseus, he was still smiling. He died knowing he had won this battle.

"That poor sap chose to die for a false sense of freedom when he could have had power. Get them both out of my sight and clean this room. Now." Commander Cobie ordered.

"Sir, the rebel still has a pulse." an officer said, loading his gun.

"Don't kill him, take him to the infirmary. He might be of some use after all." Commander Cobie said, smiling.

Chapter Twenty

Double Agent or Trader

“Sir Odysseus is dead and was of no help. Now, what do you want us to do?” commander Cobie stated.

“Your only worry is that Odysseus is dead, and that is all. Now go burn down towns, take small children, put bounties out on their heads!!! They have a weak spot. It is their people they are trying so hard to protect and set free. Threaten them, and the rebellion will come. You better find them, or I will have you joining Officer William. I mean it, Commander Cobie. Oh yes, find the mole that has been helping them and kill whoever it is." Dictator Charles warned, turning off the chat.

"Sir, I just spoke with a town's person, and they think that they saw Rocky. We all know where he is, and the others are nearby. Would you like me to send some agents to check it out?" Blake, who was dressed in full camo, informed Commander Cobie.

"Yes, I would. Get right on that, Blake." Commander Cobie replied.

"Yes, sir. Would you like to come to see the sorry looks on their faces?" Blake asked.

"Yes, go get the hummers ready to go." Commander Cobie said as Blake walked out. He pulled out a walkie-talkie.

"Oakra, are you there?" Blake asked.

"Yes, we are. What is it, Blake? Do you know where they are holding Odysseus?" Oakra asked.

"Well, he was not anymore. Look, they are going to a small town south of here to find you. So go east like we had planned. I bought you a little time but not much." Blake said.

"Ok, but what did you mean by not anymore?" Oakra asked.

"They killed him from what I have heard. I am sorry to tell you." Blake said, turning off the walkie-talkie.

When he walked up to the hummers, he made sure they were all ready to go. "Are we ready to move out yet?" Commander Cobie asked, standing behind Blake.

"Yes, sir," Blake answered swiftly.

"Good because if we don't catch them because you cause us to fall behind again, you will be saying hello to Officer Willian." Commander Cobie threatened, climbing into the hummer.

"Sir, I have another tip on another group east of here. Would you like me to check it out?" Blake asked, hoping that Commander Cobie would believe it.

"Yes, but take Delilah, will you." Commander Cobie responded.

Delilah was 5'3", with brown hair, blond highlights, and her eyes were a light green.

"Yes, sir," Blake replied.

"Delilah, come here. Please." Commander Cobie asked.

"Yes, father," Delilah replied.

"Don't let Blake out of your sight. I don't trust that boy." Commander Cobie said.

"I will not let you down, father," Delilah said, walking over to Blake.

"Delilah, please don't let me down." Commander Cobie said, watching Blake climb in a dark blue hummer.

"Delilah, are you coming? We need to get going before it gets dark. The town is a little over two hours away." Blake asked, starting the hummer.

The road Blake traveled was lined by woods on both sides and had five bridges separated by ten miles. Then the road was broken in some spots and was extremely curvy. It was about an hour when Blake pulled up to the gas station and shut off the hummer.

"What do you think you are doing? We need to get there before the rebellion gets any farther away. Are you even listening to a word I say?" Delilah asked, staring at Blake, waiting for an answer.

"Yes, but it is not going to do us any good for the hummer to run out of gas, but if you insist, we can keep driving and run out of gas halfway, then you could explain it to your father when we have to walk back." Blake explained, "Plus, I am going to the restroom."

Blake waited till he got to the bathroom, locked the door, and turned on the sink before pulling out his walkie-talkie to warn the others.

"Oakra, are you there?" Blake asked very nervously. "Yes, Blake, what is it?" Oakra asked.

"Commander Cobie sent Delilah with me. I believe he thinks that I'm the mole." Blake answered, listening at the door for Delilah.

"Ok. Take a deep breath and relax. Why do you think that?" Rocky asked.

"Hang on, who is Delilah?" Oakra asked.

"Delilah is Commander Cobie's daughter and is the best soldier in our rank. What am I going to do now?" Blake replied.

"Blake!!! Will you hurry up! I have already paid for the gas and pumped. We need to get moving. They already had a good lead on us, and now they are probably gone!" Delilah yelled, banging on the bathroom door.

When Blake opened the door, he saw Delilah tapping her foot. "Come on, we best get going," Blake replied.

"Yes. We better, how long you took." Delilah said, walking out the door, following Blake.

When Blake and Delilah had reached the next town, it was in flames, and the War State soldiers were shooting people in the streets.

"No. Please have mercy. Please stop." a woman pelted with another commander.

"What in the world is going on here?" Delilah asked.

"I don't know, let's go and find out," Blake replied, parking the hummer.

"What do you think you are doing, commander? Tell your men to stand down now." Delilah ordered, standing between him and the woman.

"I am here under the command of the great ruler Kamimir. So, I must ask you to leave Miss Delilah." The Commander said.

"If you do this, you strike fear into our people. We are here to keep the peace and protect them. This is what will cause them to rebel. To prevent that, we must have their trust." Delilah said, looking around at the people in the town who were terrified.

"Look here, little girl, one of the rulers gave the order, and your father gave us the location. So, if you don't move, I will have you executed for territory. If I was you, I would have moved." the commander yelled louder and louder.

"You think this is Justice! You believe this is a good way to create order! Well, it is not! I will not stand aside for you to kill innocent people and burn towns to the ground! This is cold-hearted and unjust! You know it. So no, I will not stand aside!" Delilah yelled back, refusing to move.

"Come on, Delilah. We can't help them." Blake said, pulling her arm as the commander lifted his gun.

"You might want to listen to your chicken friend. He has a point." the commander said, waving his gun to the side.

"Then shoot me. I will not move, Blake. If we move, he will shoot the woman." Delilah snapped and paused, "So let him shoot me. It will not do him any good, but I will not move."

With that, the commander shot her in the chest. Then turned around and shot the woman multiple times. Then turned back to Blake, lowering his gun.

"You get rid of her body. Go, dump it. I will tell her father that she was shot by a rebel. Go now!" the Commander ordered.

Blake quickly picked up Delilah and raced to the hummer. As he was speeding away, he switched the signal on the CB to match the one Oakra was using.

"Oakra! Oakra, are you there?!" Blake Stammered, looking down at Delilah to see if she was still alive.

"What is wrong, Blake?" Oakra asked.

"I need your help; Commander Cobie's daughter was shot," Blake replied, turning down a gravel road.

"Wait a minute; you want us to help the kid of a man who has been hunting us for four and a half years. I can't be the only one who sees a problem with this." Rocky pointed out.

"She died protecting a woman that one of the commanders tried to shoot. Plus, he thinks she is dead and is going to say you guys shot her." Blake remarked, speeding up.

"Ok. Just calm down and slow down. If you wreck before you get here, it will not do anyone any good." Oakra replied, preparing a place to put her.

Blake pulled up and waited for them to get Delilah out. "What are you doing?" Rocky asked.

"Getting rid of the hummer. If they find it, they might find us." Blake responded.

"Be careful, brother. Don't make me have to hunt you down." Oakra replied.

"Ok, will do. I am going to make it look like an accident." Blake said, driving off.

"Rocky, and Yash you two get rags. Jack, please find a needle and thread. Julius, you go and get medical supplies. Blaze, you get Ace so she can take care of Delilah. Right?" Oakra ordered.

Once Blake got back, he saw how worried the others were.

"Why were they burning down such a small town?" Oakra asked. "Trying to draw you guys out into the open," Blake explained.

"Well, that is great. Just great. Let's hope Delilah is willing to help us and not run and tell her daddy where we are at." Blaze growled.

"How is Delilah?" Blake asked.

"Ace said she will be fine. We are keeping an eye on her, though. Don't let your guard down." Oakra replied, "If the War States find out that she is still alive, they will kill her and us."

Three days later, Delilah woke up.

"Where am I?" Delilah asked, looking around for Blake.

"Good you awake now," Blake exclaimed.

"Where are we?" Delilah asked, looking around at the camp. "It is nice to see you are awake, Miss. Delilah," Oakra said.

"Who are you?" Delilah asked, startled.

"Delilah do not freak out. This is Oakra." Blake said calmly.

"She is one of the rebellion leaders! What on earth were you thinking? They are traders! We cannot trust them! Why did you bring us here? Why did you ask these traders for help?!" Delilah asked angrily.

"Where do I start? How about Oakra is my sister. You are supposed to be dead. Oh yes, and you are concerned about a trader because of the stunt in the town. If any War States troops catch you alive, they will torture you until you die. So, the way I see it, you have no other choice but to trust us." Blake snapped.

"Wait, Cassie. The dead sister?" Delilah asked, turning to Oakra.

"Yeah, everyone thinks I died trying to escape Mrs. Queens academy. The same will be for you. I am sorry, but you can't go home." Oakra explained.

"You can? Right?" Delilah asked, turning to Blake.

"Then what am I to tell your father?" Blake asked.

"Well, he would know that I was shot and killed. So, nothing." Delilah replied.

"Yeah, there is an issue with that, they think we are both dead. I crashed the hummer then blew it up. So, it would look like I crashed and died on the way to dispose of your body." Blake explained.

"And there is one more problem with that. We no longer have anyone on the inside. How are we going to know what they are planning?" Rocky replied, looking at the others.

"I don't know, but we better figure out something before they burn any more towns down. They have already burned down four more towns. We need a plan and fast." Oakra said.

"What if we turn them against each other?" Blaze asked. "How in the world are we going to do that?" Ace asked.

"Well, I don't know, but if we can, that will make it easier on us." Blaze replied.

"That is true." Ace said.

"How are we going to do that? Is still a big question." Rocky replied.

"Ok, how about we feed the fire between Russia and Germany." Oakra responded, looking at Delilah. "How?" Rocky asked.

"By feeding the fire Germany started," Oakra said. "What does that mean?" Delilah asked.

"Oakra is right. Think about it. The German commander shot, and as far as anyone knows, they killed Russia's best fighter on top of her being Commander Cobie's kid. We just need to give it another push. Think of it like throwing gasoline on a fire." Blake explained.

"The only problem is turning that fire into a forest fire." Delilah cut in. "Blake is going to hack into the system and fire a missile at the Russia base. Then Russia, in return, will fire back at Germany. They will be so busy fighting back and forth with each other. This will force

President Linna to step in. While they are fighting with each other, they will not realize that it is us causing it. When their numbers are weaker, we will finish them off." Oakra explained.

"Ok, but what if that does not work? What if President Linna does not intervene? What if they find out it is us?" Delilah asked.

"Look, I know that it is a lot of what-ifs. Our only chance is to get them to fight each other even if we can't get them all fighting each other. We have a plan b. If needed." Oakra said looking at Delilah.

"Ok. What is plan b?" Delilah asked, looking puzzled.

"I think it is best you don't know what it is." Oakra implied.

Chapter Twenty One

A House Divided Can Not Stand

"So, are you this will fuel the fire?" Jack asked.

"Yes! Just stay out of sight." Oakra replied.

"Ok, are you sure we can trust Delilah?" Jack asked, climbing through the vents.

"Yes, I am sure we can trust her." Oakra answered, "Now keep quiet,"

After Jack and Oakra got back to camp, they handed Katheran a file labeled top secret.

"Ok, so now what is the file for again?" Jack asked.

"We are going to place the files in my father's hummer, so the German troops think that the Russian troops took it. Then we are going to take some of the uniforms from each war state sector and shoot at the vehicles to cause them to fight back and forth at each other so Blake can hack into the missiles and fire at the War States main bases, which will force President Linna to get involved. Afterward, we can go and clean up the mess and take back the United States." Delilah explained.

"Will these files and firing at them in opposite uniforms cause them to fight long enough for Blake to hack their missiles?" Julius asked.

"Good point, we could take out some of the commanders while wearing the opposite uniform. This way, they will think the other sector wants to take the other's land." Delilah suggested.

"That might work. Then to push them over the edge just far enough, we could shoot and miss one of their leaders. All of that will cause a big enough fire to cause them to fight. Then maybe we will not have to hack the missiles to fire them. Just change the coordinates of the missile." Oakra replied.

"What? Why?" Jack asked, puzzled.

"I get it if we do that, they will fire them on their own. This will make it easier for Blake to hack their systems, and harder for them to trace us." Ziggy replied.

"Then once they have fired at each other a few times, Blake will hack the systems and fire one at President Linna's land. That will force her hand." Rocky explained.

"Next, while their attention is on each other, we will meet up with Saturn and the rest of the rebellion," Blake suggested.

"We will split into two groups. A small group will go to the white house to clear out the civilians before the second group will move in once the civilians run away. Once we all are there, we will take back the white house and end this war of chaos." Oakra explained.

It was a few days later after the files were placed in Commander Cobie's hummer. That caused a small fight but not enough to do much, so they went to phase two of the plan. Phase two was the rebellion would dress up in the German and Russian uniforms and shoot at them, making sure that the only thing seen was the uniform. This caused them to fight a little more, which meant it was finally time for phase three.

"Ace, are you in place?" Delilah asked, watching Kazeimir through her scop.

Delilah was lying on a cliff that sat where you could see everything. She was laying on a pile of leaves near an old oak tree for cover. Delilah made sure she was wearing gloves so she could leave the gun where it was and make it appear as if a troop had rushed out.

"Yes, I am in place waiting on Oakra's signal." Ace answered, looking at Dictator Charles through a sniper scope lining up the shoot so the bullet would fire above his head.

Ace was hiding out in a cave on the side of some bluffs, looking over the town where dictator Charles was giving a speech. Ace had gloves on as well, so she could leave the gun, but she was also ditching a German uniform and a bag, so it seemed as if she changed to blend into the crowd.

"Fire, if you both have the shots, but make sure you don't kill them; we need them to unlock the missiles for the plan to work," Oakra replied.

With that, they both slowly pulled the triggers on the guns, knowing they would have to make sure the ruthless dictators lived.

"Shot fired. I'm out." Ace responded, standing up and leaving. "Same here, see you guys at the rondeau," Delilah replied, slipping into the cover of the woods.

"How dare they try to kill me!!! That is a direct threat!! It is an act of war!!! Arm our missiles, and let's return the favor!!" Kazeimir ordered.

"Sir are you sure this will break the treaty with President Linna." a troop warned.

"Of course, I am sure I don't care about that treaty! I got what I wanted! Now fire you fool, or I will have your head!!" Kazeimir yelled.

The missile hit one of the smaller military bases for the Russian sector.

"First, they killed one of our best soldiers. Then they opened fire at my troops for no reason. Afterward, they attempt to kill me. Now they are firing missiles at us. Return the favor and take them out, starting with the biggest base they have." Dictator Charles demanded.

"It will be my pleasure, sir." Commander Cobie replied with a slight smirk because it was payback time.

This continued back and forth for three days before being brought to President Linna's attention.

"Madam, I am sorry to interrupt, but Russia and Germany are still firing missiles at each other. Plus, the treaty you had with them has been broken. One of their missiles was fired at one of our bases. What do you want us to do?" security Smith asked, looking at the anger forming on her face.

"They what!!!!! I want missiles fired at both bases. Then bring me the pathetic leaders and their commanders!! They will pay for this!! Time to make an example out of them!!" President Linna yelled, snapping her pencil.

"Yes, madam. I will have it done right away." Security Smith replied, leaving the room.

"Alexander. Bring me, Blake. I want him alive." President Linna responded.

"Madam, he is dead. He crashed his Hummer trying to save someone in the Russian army." Security Smith replied.

"Ok, very well then. Have Dr. Juno moved to prison two, and I want an update on her son Oscar as soon as possible." President Linna said, waving him out.

"We did it. They are fighting so much that President Linna was forced to step in! Now that's what I am talking about!" Nightshade cheered.

"Don't get cocky, Nightshade, that is only part of the plan. We still have a long way to go to win this war." Oakra responded, sharpening her caber.

"Oh! Come on, Oakra cut loose. We have gotten this far. Have some fun." Yash replied.

"Oakra is right, don't get too far ahead of yourselves. We still have to take out President Linna." Rocky reminded them, walking past them.

"You two are party poopers. You know this right." Blaze replied.

"Just have a little fun. We have nothing to do but wait out for a bit." Blake responded.

"Yeah, Cassie, come on, please come and join us." Ziggy Jumped in.

"No thanks, you guys can if you want, but don't get loud. We don't need to get caught." Oakra replied, "Now I am going to bed. Don't be up to late."

"Oakra and Rocky are right. This war has yet to be won. Don't get cocky." Delilah responded, walking to her sleeping bag.

"Have they always been like that?" Luke asked, looking around the fire Pit.

"I don't know about the other two, but no, Oakra was not always like this." Blake answered.

"What do you mean?" Luke asked.

"Before world war three broke out, we lived in the white house. She went by Cassie back then. Once, our father was shot, for the first time, he sent me to stay with Commander Cobie. As for Cassie, she was sent to live at Mrs. Queens academy. That is when she started to change a little bit at a time. That is also when she met Ziggy. Once they escaped after the war, Cassie showed how much she had changed. From that day on, she has gone by Oakra." Blake explained to Luke.

"Oh! I didn't know," Luke replied.

"Don't feel bad, kid hardly anyone did," Blaze responded.

After that, Ziggy got up and went to bed.

"The only one who did know what caused Cassie to change to Oakra is Ziggy. Neither one of them talk about it, though." Nightshade replied.

"Oh!" Luke said, looking at both of them.

"But hey, they will have your back no matter what. Trust me on that." Julius exclaimed.

12/23/2024

It has been almost three years since anyone has called me Cassie. I didn't realize how much I would miss that name, but Cassie died the day we got free. It took the War States four years to build their kingdom on the people's misery and only three weeks to tear them apart at the seams. We found the loose thread and pulled at it. Now before their very eyes, they are tearing each other apart instead of talking. Just what we were hoping. A house that is divided cannot stand. It is time to take this war to them.

While they have weakened each other, we have grown stronger. I believe it is time for them to leave our country. This is the land of the free and the home of the brave. Their chaos is no longer welcomed here. President Linna will pay for everything she has done. So will her mindless lap dogs. This is our home and the people's country. We will end this war or die trying.

Cassie

Chapter Twenty Two

The President Is On Top

"**M**adam, we have killed all except for Kazeimir, Charles, and Commander Cobie. The other commanders were already dead by the time we reached their headquarters." Security Smith informed President Linna, "What do you want me to do with them?"

"I am going to execute them publicly to make an example of them." President Linna replied.

"Yes, madam. I will have the ropes ready." Security Smith responded. "No. I want them to suffer slowly and painfully for double-crossing me. So, I want; boiling water, two syringes, rattlesnake venom, my hammer, and one of their guns. Use the barbed wire to restrain them to the chair. Gather as many people as possible. It is time this country learns to fear me." President Linna replied, waving Security Smith out of the room.

Meanwhile, the rebellion had got wind of this. They met up with Saturn and the rest of the rebellion to get ready to fight.

"Ok, Rocky, Blaze, Blake, and Delilah are with me. The rest of you will stay here with Ziggy, Nightshade, Saturn, and Ace. Wait for our signal. If we get caught, regroup and go to plan B. No civilians are to be hurt." Oakra ordered, "We have less than two hours until she shows her true colors. That is when we make our move."

"Everything has to go as planned. One slip up, and we will get caught and loose." Rocky explained

It was an hour before the execution, and President Linna was deciding what to wear. She had four outfits laid across her bed. The first outfit was a dark grey jacket with a white blouse, dark grey pants, and grey shoes with long white socks, the second one was a black dress with a pearl necklace and black heels, and the third was a light blue shirt and skirt. The final outfit was a white dress with a red belt, a red jacket, and red high heels.

"Which one do you think I should wear tonight?" President Linna asked an older cleaning maid.

"The white one, madam. It shows the power and will bring out your eyes. Plus, it will prove to the people you are not scared to get your hands dirty bringing justice and order." The older lady answered calmly.

"Ok, thank you for the advice. You are free to leave now." President Linna replied, dismissing the maid.

The older maid stepped into the hallway and left to find Security Smith to let him know that the tools were ready, and the prisoners were being restrained as they spoke.

"Ok, ladies and gentlemen. You see these three scum bags. These are the ones who double-crossed us and broke my laws. Let them serve as an example of what will happen to any further rebellion or attacks against my country." President Linna announced to the crowd of people as she showed the three men restrained to chairs with barbed wire.

Their hands were bleeding from them, trying to struggle. The pants legs were all torn from the barbed wire, and they had bruises from when the guards had to bring them in by force. She had them displayed on the stage with red curtains. No one noticed that Oakra and her group had slipped into the crowd. Each one of them had a smoke bomb to set off to cause the civilians to panic and run. The only problem was they all saw who was on the stage. Their attention immediately went toward Delilah, who was frozen in fear.

The first one up for execution was Kazeimir. President Linna picked up the syringe filled with gently altered rattlesnake venom. This venom took effect faster and caused ten times more pain than normal venom. Once she had injected him with the venom, it took three minutes before his arm began to turn black. As Kazeimir started to scream in pain at the same time, President Linna began to smile.

Then once she had watched Kazeimir suffer for a bit, she moved on to Charles. She ran her hand across the tray until she reached the syringe filled with water that was 300 degrees Fahrenheit. The needle itself was putting off heat. As she began to place the syringe into Charles's arm, he screamed in pain. Within seconds he was dead, and so was Kazeimir.

The last one was Commander Cobie. As he looked up, he saw Delilah watching in terror. Behind him stood

President Linna holding his gun, ready to shoot him. While no one else noticed, Blake ran up, behind her grabbing her arm to try and turn her away.

"Since you were only taking orders, I will give you the chance to say any last words." President Linna said, stepping beside him.

"I am sorry I was wrong to help your cause, Linna. If I could redo it, I would have stopped you from the beginning. I am sorry, Delilah." Commander Cobbie replied, looking into the crowd, "but I will not beg for mercy."

As he said his final words, President Linna pulled the trigger. His chair fell backward, and blood splattered all over her white dress. At that moment, Delilah broke free and ran toward the stage.

"NO. Dad. I am so sorry this is my fault." Delilah wept as Blake caught her before she got to the stage.

This drew President Linna's attention to them. She slowly walked down the steps and had the guards move toward them. Rushing to their side were Oakra, Rocky, and Blaze. They all had their weapons drawn ready for a fight.

"So, you three are alive, nice to know. Now I understand the pieces fit together perfectly. I didn't have any real problems until you supposedly died trying to escape, Cassie. Blake, for shame, I gave you access to the best tech in the world, and you used it to free useless people. Then there is you, Delilah, one of the best fighters I have ever seen turned by such a small act." President Linna sighed, "Such a shame I could have used you guys. So much potential wasted."

"Yeah, I am alive and have been the thorn in your side. I told you that you would not get away with anything. You killed my father, Robert, Odysseus, and Jove, then on top of that, you turned the land of the free into chaos with you at the top," Oakra replied, ready to fire her bow.

"You learned no manners when you were with Mrs. Queens. Now I will not kill you guys as long as you surrender now. So do we have a deal?" President Linna responded, looking at Oakra.

"Go to hell; I am not surrendering to a devil-like you," Oakra replied.

"Drop dead; I have been there and done that," Rocky remarked.

"So, what. We are with them on this." Blake and Blaze jumped in.

"I surrender." Delilah sobbed and leaned over to hug Blake, "Trust me , I have a plan."

"Well, at least one of you children has some common sense. Kill the rest." President Linna said, looking at the rest of them.

"You backstabbing traitor!!!" Rocky yelled as Blake grabbed him. "Madam, can we give them a try? I think that would help them to earn the people's respect." Delilah suggested, looking at President Linna.

"You are right. We will have a trial to find a more suitable punishment than death. If I break the leaders, the rest will fall." President Linna agreed.

"Come play along, Delilah said to trust her," Blake whispered, letting go of Rocky.

"Fine, we will go quietly." Blaze replied, putting her hands up.

As the guards walked them to their cells, the five began to fight to make it seem more believable.

"This is your fault." Rocky snapped at Blake.

"My fault!! You had a gun! You could have used it, so you are to blame as well!" Blake snapped.

"You both are to blame you for this one forever trusting Delilah and the other for not shooting anyone when you had the chance." Blaze remarked.

"Knock it off; it is all of our fault for not catching her fast enough and bringing her with us knowing it was a possibility. She is just scared, that's all." Oakra snapped at all of them.

"Maybe we should have knocked them out first." a younger guard remarked.

"I agree with that." an older guard replied, walking behind them.

"Yes, then they would be quieter, but then we would be forced to pack all of them to their cells." a third guard pointed out.

Once they were taken to their cells, the guards made sure every other cell was locked, so they could not get free.

"Do you really think these are going to hold us?" Oakra challenged the guards.

"Yes, I know it will hold you, prisoners, until trial." the younger guard replied.

"You know who she is? Right? She is one of two who escaped from Mrs. Queens academy. So, I don't think this will hold us." Rocky jumped in, what Oakra was doing.

"Oh! really. I am so scared of some little girl stuck behind bars." the younger guard replied.

"You should be. When I get out, you will be the one to get my calling card first." Oakra warned.

"Will you just shut up already? You are driving me crazy." the younger guard snapped, stepping away from Oakra's cell.

"She is playing you for weakness. Ignore them before President Linna hears you yelling at Carson's daughter. This one has caused nothing but trouble from day one." the older guard warned.

12/25/2024

Well, things have officially gone south. We managed to take out the War States, which left President Linna. Somehow, we didn't think bringing Delilah to her father's execution was a bad idea. Now we have to trust that Delilah and the others can bail us out. Otherwise, we are on our own. This is still better than the academy, though. The younger guard seems to be aggravated easily. I think if he gets mad enough, he will not notice if we take his key card. Hopefully, things don't get worse, but with our luck, they might.

Cassie

Chapter Twenty Three

The Trail

The guards walked Oakra and the others to a clearing not far from where the execution took place. There stood President Linna under an old maple tree that was dying. Proving she could care less about anyone or anything that didn't benefit her in some way. The grass around it was brown and yellow.

"This is your last chance. Will you take it or become slaves in one way or the other?" President Linna asked, "What will it be, Cassie?"

"The name is Oakra now and drop dead. I will never obey those who wish to create chaos. I will uprise and rebel against them and fight for what is right." Oakra challenged President Linna.

"The rest of you wish to join her, or will you follow Delilah?" President Linna asked, looking at the rest, who nodded their heads at each other.

"Together we stand!" the other three replied, staring her down. "If it is together you stand, then it will be together you will break."

President Linna replied, "Send Blake and this young lady to the fields and send Cassie and this man to the pits. I want them all out of my sight in one week."

"That was no trail, Linna, and you know it. The sad part is you were foolish enough to broadcast this so-called trial. Where is the judge or the jury? The only thing this proves is that you are no better than the other dictators that you executed in front of everyone. You are worse because you lied to everyone by telling them that you were here to protect them. Well, I have a secret of yours, and I think it is time that the people should know who was the true corrupt one in this government. It was you who created the super virus, Echidna. You are the one who ordered the plane to be shot down, and it was you who had my father killed. You only wanted power, and in gaining it, you took away the people's freedom. Here is you wake up, call your secrets out, and this is the land of the free. Let's see you hold the order now." Oakra exposed her on live TV with a smile, knowing that there was no way for her to hide her lies now.

"You spoiled little brat!!! You will pay for that!!!!" President Linna snapped, shooting Oakra to silence her, "Now get them out of my sights and turn off that damn camera!!!!!"

"Oakra!!!!!!!" Blake screamed, catching her before she hit the ground.

"Great, Oakra got shot and is not waking up, and we are stuck in a damn cell and also have no clue what is going on outside of these walls!!! Does no one believe in bringing us any medical supplies!!! No, they don't because they are all idiotic couriers!!!" Rocky yelled, pacing the cell that they were all locked in.

"Rocky, for Blake's sake, maybe we cool it just a bit. The two of us need to stay calm because someone has to find a way out of this mess." Blaze suggested turning to Blake, who was sitting beside Oakra.

"Yeah, you should be glad we are letting you all in the same cell." the younger guard remarked, standing against the bars.

"Rocky, don't! We can't afford two of you guys getting shot. Oakra did us a favor. She revealed President Linna's true colors, and there is no way she can hide that now. That will cause more people to rebel against her. So, cool it because if she wakes up to find you let your temper get the best of you, and you got shot because of it, she will beat the living hell out of you." Blake ordered, standing up, "We will get out, and each one of you sorry assholes will pay."

"Whatever you say, young man, but I don't fear the computer hacker. Face it, your leader is out for the count. None of you are a true threat without her." the older guard replied with a chuckle.

"That is what you think, but those berries your buddy over there has been eating for the last hour are poisonous. I give it ten minutes until he begins to vomit, five more before he gets the runs, and then another ten before he dies. Give or take a few minutes because he was eating them when we came back." Blaze grinned.

"Yeah, right, young lady. You are bluffing." the older guard replied.

Within five minutes, the guard began to vomit, and then he got the runs just like Blaze said. Soon afterward, he collapsed from fever and died.

"See, here is the problem with thinking Oakra is the only threat in the room. That was my bag. Those berries are turned into the poison that her arrows are covered in and the same poison we use for our knives." Blaze informed the remaining guards, "So who else was foolish enough to eat them?"

"You have these; that means you know how to stop it!!" one of the guards snapped, right before he began to vomit.

"You're right, I do, but there are seven other poison berries in the bag and six more deadly plants. There is only one plant to stop the effects. So this is how this is going to work. You will get Oakra the medical supplies, and I will tell you which one will stop the effects. Now you could shoot me too, but then you will definitely die." Blaze replied, "Do we have a deal or not?"

"There is no need for that. Here I brought you some." Security Smith responded, walking to the cell.

"Yeah, and how do we know you didn't poison these?" Rocky questioned.

"Look, you have every right not to trust me, I understand, but please believe me that I would not do a thing to harm Cassie." Security Smith pleated, trying to help.

"Why should we trust you? You work for that devil in the white house." Rocky replied.

"Because his name is Alexander, and he is our uncle. He helped raise us after our mother was shot." Blake answered, looking at Oakra, "she doesn't like being called Cassie anymore. It is Oakra. Tell the guards the plant, but if you choose to double-cross our family or not, you will pay for it dearly."

"Blake, I never told you that. How did you know?" Alexander asked, treating Oakra's wound, "she got lucky it barely missed her heart."

"I had access to the best tech. I ran a few tests and did some digging. You are our mother's half-brother. It made sense that you stuck around after she died when dad needed your help." Blake answered, sitting back down by Oakra.

"I spoke with President Linna. She is going to wait until Oakra can fight before she sends any of you guys away. To avoid any form of rebellion until you are away from her white house. I know it is not much, but it is the best I could do." Alexander informed them.

After a few days, Oakra woke up.

"oww. What happened?" Oakra asked, sitting up and looking around.

"Cassie!!" Blake yelled, jumping up and hugging her.

"You almost died again. I said for you not to do that again?" Rocky replied.

"My bad. I didn't think the lunatic would shoot me herself." Oakra responded, standing up, "We are still in this hell hole?"

"Yep, we are here until you can fight back, then Blake and Blaze will be sent to the fields, and you and I will be sent to the pits. Didn't think I would end up there again." Rocky answered.

"Great. Wait, why there are less guards?" Oakra replied. "They ate some of Blaze's poison berries, and we refused to help them until they helped us," Blake answered.

"Ok," Oakra replied.

"So now what?" Blaze asked, looking at Oakra.

"Well, we need to think outside the box. They are giving us an army and don't even know it." Oakra replied, "Time to play the hand we were dealt. The fields and pits are the largest groups of prisoners they have, and we now have access inside."

"I get it," Rocky replied.

1/08/2025

I was out for two weeks and woke up and finally figured out a way to win this war. President Linna is literally giving us two armies and doesn't even notice her mistake. On top of that, I get told that the worrywart Alexander Smith is my uncle. That explains why he stayed by dad's side. It has now been five years of the War States in charge, but President Linna's ignorance will be what causes her to fall. We stand together.

Cassie

Chapter Twenty Four

Fields of Blood

"So, you are the new slave here." An older man said.

The old man had grey hair, blue eyes, and was 5'7" with a boney build. He was wearing old torn-up clothes that were a little short.

"I am no one's slave," Blake replied, meeting the man's eyes.

"You're right; no slave would have dared chanced to look someone in the eyes after mouthing off like that." the older man responded, looking at Blake, "So do you not have a name, or is it just a lack of manners kid?"

"The name is Blake. Now, who are you?" Blake answered.

"So, it is a lack of manners. My name is Alden." the old man snickered.

"Well, I see you have met the old man. By the way, the guards are going to love that attitude. The name is Hestia." a girl with raven hair and blue eyes jumped in.

"So, it will be fun ticking them off. Good." Blake replied with a smile.

"Hold your horses' young man, don't go acting like you are in the rebellion now. That is a good way to get yourself killed around here." Alden warned, shaking his head, knowing what was about to happen.

"Please, listen to Alden," Hestia replied, grading his arm as a guard walked past.

"Well. Well. If it isn't Blake, the rebellion leader's little brother. You best behave, or you will regret it," a guard commented and walked past.

"So much for keeping you out of trouble." Alden remarked, beginning to work once more, "Just keep your head down for a while."

"So, you are Mr. Rebellion. Well, let me show you around. Over there are the housing units. Off to the left of us is where we all eat. The two boys over there are my brothers. The smaller one with raven hair is my twin, Agni. The larger one with dirty blond hair is my older brother Calder." Hestia greeted Blake.

"Look, kid, it is best just to get your work done and keep your head down. From what I heard, the guards already know who you are, and your sister is not going to be able to bail you out this time." Calder warned.

"Calder is right, so stay out of trouble, kid," Agni replied.

"Ok, noted," Blake responded, knowing that was not going to work very well.

The next day, they went to work in the fields. The crop in this field was rice. It was time to harvest the crop. All of the people working the fields kept their heads down to avoid getting any lashes from the guards. Each one of the guards was riding a horse and had a whip on the horn of the saddle. As Blake started to harvest the rice, he saw Hestia fall backward as a guard raised his whip to hit her.

Pop! Blake had stepped in front of her. The whip had caught Blake across his arm.

"You choose to help this worthless slave at your own cost that will cost you, young man." the guard remarked, raising his whip as another slammed Blake to the ground, "ten lashings should do it."

After the guards left, Agni and Calder helped him to the housing units, while Hestia went to find Alden.

"What in the world did you do to get ten lashes on your first day?" Agni asked, helping get his shirt off so they could clean and bandage his wounds.

"He was stupid and stopped the whip from hitting me. That made the guard mad." Hestia answered.

"Where is Alden?" Calder asked, carefully whipping the cuts from the whip, "Anyways, thank you for saving our sister."

"Awe! No problem. Are you ok?" Blake replied.

"I am fine, thanks to you. Although I think the guards have it out for you. Normally, if something like that happens, they go on their way, but I guess with you being in the rebellion, they will not change it." Hestia responded.

"Good to know." Blake chuckled, "Awe!"

"Stop your bellyaching, kid. I told you to keep your head down. No matter what, but did you listen?" Alden remarked, walking into the door with the medical supplies, "How many Lashes? Two or three?"

"Try about ten Lashes. The guards really don't like him." Agni answered.

"So, it appears that way," Alden responded, looking at his wounds.

"Eleven counting his arm," Hestia replied, lifting his arm to show them.

After two hours, Alden had finished and sent Blake to bed.

"He is going to get a lot of those. The guards know he is willing to take a hit for someone else, and that is all they need." Alden warned the other three, "Keep an eye on him and make sure his wounds don't get infected."

"Will do, Alden. Thank you," Hestia replied.

The next three days were hell for Blake; the guards had him doing extra work with less food and water because of the stunt with Hestia. Then Blake saw a little girl with brown hair and hazel eyes crying in the field and another guard. This girl was clean and didn't look like a slave, but the guard still raised his whip to her. Blake raced over to her, using himself as a shield. The whip cracked across his back. This caught everybody's attention. No one would have been willing to take a beating once for someone else, but twice now.

"You again? You can't help but play hero, don't you?" the guard asked, raising the whip not giving Blake the chance to react, "this time, I will see to it that you don't try this again. 30 lashes should do it."

After the guard was finished Blake let the little girl down. Knowing she was not going to get hit again.

"Are you ok?" Blake asked the little girl.

Everyone stared in shock. Blake stopped the whip from hitting the head guard's daughter and took a beating for it. Without thinking twice, Blake once again made himself the guards' main target.

"Yes, thank you. That guard will pay, I promise. Daddy will hear about this." the little girl answered, "what is your name? My name is Ruby."

"Blake is my name and ok," Blake replied, struggling to get up. "Hang on, hotshot. Let us help you." Hestia responded, helping him up as Ruby ran toward a big grey and green house.

"You just can't help yourself, can you?" Calder chuckled, helping Blake from the other side.

"Come on, you, fool, let's get you back to the house and patch you up." Hestia replied, "Agni go find Alden, tell him we need his help again."

"Ok, Hestia," Angi responded, running to find Alden.

"Well, you couldn't keep your head down, could you? Now, look at you. You can barely walk, kid. When will you learn?" Alden asked, walking over to look at his back.

"So, you are the one I have to thank for stopping the whip from hitting my little girl?" a guard asked, standing in the doorway, "My name is Bearach."

Bearach was 6'1" with a slime build. He had blond hair and grayish-blue eyes.

"Yes, sir. He is the one you have to thank for that." Alden replied. "How bad is his back, Alden?" Bearach asked.

"Come and look. If you really want to thank the boy, you might want to start with medical supplies. So, I can patch him up. Then the guard did this because he chose to protect your daughter." Alden replied.

"Awe!" Blake responded as Alden wiped a rag across his back.

"I will have the guard punished for this and get some more medical supplies for you. Stay in bed for a few days." Bearach crunched as he saw Blake's back, "Wait, those ones look a little older. Did this happen before?"

"Yes. Three days ago. He stopped the whip from hitting me. It was the same guard." Hestia answered.

"Then why was he not in bed then?" Bearach questioned.

"Because he is bullheaded and doesn't listen to us," Agni answered.

"Oh yes, you must be Blake. Oakra's little brother." Bearach replied, "This is an order to get some rest. I don't want to see you in the field for a few days."

"We will make sure he stays in bed for a while," Calden responded.

"All done. It only took four hours to patch you up this time. Now go to bed. Calden, help him to bed." Alden said, cleaning the mess from it.

"Awe! Thank you, Alden." Blake responded as he stood up.

"I have seen that look before, Alden. What are you thinking?" Hestia asked, watching Calder help Blake to bed.

"He might be the one to get you guys out of here." Alden replied, "Make sure he gets some rest. President Linna is coming in two days, and she is the one who sent him here."

"Yes, sir," Hestia responded.

"So, you are Oakra's little brother? Wait, if you are Carson's son, that means Oakra is Cassie?" Calder asked.

"Awe! Yeah, Oakra is Cassie, but she doesn't like to be called Cassie anymore." Blake answered.

Two days later, Blake went back to working in the fields. Right then, a solid white car came flying down the road in between the fields. It was President Linna and Delilah.

"Blake. Have you learned your lesson? Will you side with me?" President Linna asked with a smile, hoping the fields had broken him.

"I thought I told you I would rather die than help you. We stand together." Blake replied.

"I can make you a commander. What can that so-called family do for you?" President Linna responded, still smiling.

"I know the only reason you are here is that you are scared of the people Oakra turned against you, and Blaze got away. So, you only have three of us, and we both know neither one of them is going to

help you. I am standing with, family. Go to hell; I am not about to become your pawn." Blake snapped.

"I gave you a chance to get out of here, and you choose the damn rebellion!" President Linna yelled, slapping him across his face, "Delilah!!! We are leaving now!!"

"So, I was right Blaze got free." Blake chuckled, standing back to his feet.

As Delilah climbed into the car, she nodded her head to verify that Blaze got freed.

"Madam, there is a little girl on the road." the driver said.

"Then run her over." President Linna replied.

Blake saw the car racing toward Ruby. He quickly leaped to his feet, the rest of the way racing the car to her. Blake grabbed her and rolled off the road and went tumbling down the hill. They came to a stop when Blake hit a rather large rock.

"Are you ok, Ruby?" Blake asked, sitting up.

"Yes. Thank you again, Blake." Ruby replied.

"Ruby, Blake, are you two, ok?" Bearach asked.

"I am fine, thanks to Blake," Ruby answered.

"Thank you, Blake. I did not think you would be the one to save a GR States guard's child knowingly. I owe you my life for that." Bearach remarked.

"Like, you said, she is a child. Hatred is something that is taught rather than something that is born." Blake answered, looking up from where he was sitting.

"You still didn't answer my question. Are you ok?" Bearach asked.

"I think so; a few cuts and bruises, but I think I am ok," Blake replied.

Little did Blake know, within a week, he was there he started to change everyone's view on how things should be done. He put others before himself and was following in Oakra's footsteps.

"You are not fine; look at your arm and wrist. Hestia and Calder take him back to the housing units. Agni, go get Alden and tell him Blake needs medical attention again." Bearach responded.

"Honestly, I'm fine, sir," Blake replied, starting to stand up.

"Dude, if you are not careful President Linna might shoot you herself," Calder warned as they walked away.

"That is if Alden does not kill you first. This makes three times in only a week." Hestia chuckled.

"Well, you can't stay out of trouble, can you? Go set him in the chair. What happened this time?" Alden remarked, meeting them at the door.

"Someone played hero again and almost got hit by President Linna's car. Then went tumbling down a hill and hit a rock." Calder answered.

"And the bruise on his cheek?" Alden questioned.

"He told President Linna off, and she slapped him," Hestia replied.

"Look, I am fine, you guys," Blake responded.

"If this is what you call fine, but your arm needs stitches, and your wrist is sprained." Alden replied, smacking Blake in the back of the head, "Now shut up and sit still."

"Is he ok?" Bearach asked.

"Yes, a few stitches and a brace, he will be ok. Why?" Alden answered.

"Good, get him patched up now. It is time for him to leave and you guys as well. President Linna just called. She will be here in a week to have him killed. You four and Ruby will be going with him for your own safety. No Ifs and buts, you guys are leaving tonight." Bearach replied, handing them a gun, "Once you take this country back, then you will free the rest of us, but for now you must run. We will buy you time. Find your sister and the rest of the rebellion. She turned the people against President Linna; now, you all need to unit them and stand together."

"Are you sure, sir?" Blake asked, "And what do you mean we will?"

"The guards and the rest of the people here are on your side." Bearach answered, shoving them out the door.

At the gate, Ruby was waiting for them with tears filling her eyes.

"Goodbye, Ruby. Daddy loves you. Take care of my little girl, Blake." Bearach said, looking at Blake.

"I will, sir," Blake replied.

With that, the six left the field plod. With Blake free, this only left Rocky and Oakra to get free. President Linna didn't know it yet but had already lost this war. The rebellion now had the numbers. Blake knew the road ahead would be long and rough, but with six new members, nothing was going to stand in their way of freedom. What they didn't know was how close Odysseus was.

Chapter Twenty Five

The Pits

"Get up. Come on, Pipsqueak, if you fall like that in the pits, you will die for sure." A well-built muscular man ordered.

"My name is not Pipsqueak!!! It is Rocky!! How many times do I have to tell you people that?!" Rocky snapped, swinging his wooden sword.

"Keep that temper in check. Anger clouds your judgment. Now run it again." the man replied.

"No, I am done here! Where is Oakra?!" Rocky snapped again.

"Look, pipsqueak Oakra is probably training like you should be doing. Tip of advice: forget who you were before this. It will get you killed." the man suggested.

"No, I won't forget it! What will get you killed is forgetting who you are and from where you came. Those make you stronger. Without that, you are no better than the War States. So no, I will not just forget it." Rocky snapped, blocking the man's sword.

"You have a lot to learn, Pipsqueak." the man chuckled.

"My name is Rocky!!!! No, I don't have a lot to learn!! You do!! Now I said I was done!!!" Rocky yelled, swinging his wooden sword with enough force that it shattered the man's sword, "Now I am going to find Oakra!"

"You are done when I say you are Pipsqueak. Not until then. Chicf, you are in the next suit for the pits." a guard replied, tapping his fingers on his gun, "now get back to training Pipsqueak."

"First off, my name is Rocky, not Pipsqueak. Second, off I am not scared of your tiny gun! The troops and guards I killed had bigger ones. Third, I know President Linna will kill you if you shoot Oakra or me before our first fight. So be my guest." Rocky remarked, leaving to find Oakra.

"Use more power and less speed. If you can't get your opponent in a few hits, the little lady will kill you." a heavily built man with black hair pointed out.

"It is not all about power. There are two sides to a coin. Power may be one, but it is useless without brains." Oakra remarked, swinging a chain around the man's feet and pulling, causing him to fall, "Oh! my name is Oakra. Not little lady. Don't forget that."

"Lunchtime rodents!" a guard yelled.

"Nole, come here," Chief said, waving over the man who was training Oakra.

"What is it?" Nole asked.

"What do you think of these rookies?" Chief asked, watching Rocky and Oakra.

"I have only worked with the girl. She does not have a lot of power but is quick on her feet and smart. What about the boy? I heard him snapping a lot." Nole replied.

"He has a lot of power but a bad temper. He snapped one of the heavy training swords today. You can tell they are not new to the game of war." Chief responded.

"If they are not careful, they will be put against each other." Nole pointed out.

"What was the girl's name?" Chief asked.

"Oakra. Why do you ask?" Nole responded.

"Great, now I get it. They are in rebellion. Oakra is the leader, and Rocky is her right hand." Chief replied.

"If that is the case, things are going to get messy around here," Nole said, looking over at them.

"I agree neither one of them fears the guards. Maybe they might be our way out." Chief pointed out with a smile.

"Oakra, have you figured a way out of here yet?" Rocky asked.

"No, I haven't, and keep it down." Oakra replied, "I have been stuck in training all day."

"Ok, let me know when you do," Rocky responded.

"Rocky, you are with me now," Nole said, walking up to their table.

"Ok." Rocky replied, looking at his feet, "you let her get a hold of a chain, didn't you?"

"What makes you say that?" Nole asked.

"Well, one, you are covered in dirt and bruises. Two, you are the only one who was training with her today." Rocky replied.

"Nice to know I am not the only one she has done that too," Nole responded.

"Yeah, she has done it to several guards and troops, but they needed a grave afterward. You are one of the few people she has not killed doing that." Rocky snickered, feeling the glare from Oakra, "Awe! Hey, I am just saying."

"Rocky, don't get us into trouble yet," Oakra ordered.

"She may be fast, but she doesn't have the power for that," Nole said.

"Wow, does she have you fooled? She uses her head more but trust me; she is tougher than she looks." Rocky chucked, "she played you like a fiddle."

"So cute but deadly," Nole replied.

"Yeah, she studies you while fighting to find weak points. Then fools someone into the harmless act." Rocky explained, "Awe!"

"Shut up, Rocky," Oakra warned after kicking him.

"I feel sorry for Chief. You are mean." Nole replied as Chief walked up.

"Little lady, I hope you aren't as short-fused as your friend here," Chief commented.

"No, she is not, but she is meaner than him," Nole warned. "Oh then, she is a redhead that is to be expected," Chief replied, walking to the training area.

"Well, isn't he just Mr. Sunshine." Oakra sassed, getting up.

The two switch back and forth between the two trainers. This did not give Oakra much time to study the building for a way out. After two weeks, they had their first suits for the pits. Oakra was up first in the pits.

The man she was put against was 6 '7 ``, with a real muscular build. He had brown hair and blue eyes. His weapon of choice was a sword. Oakra decided that her best bet would be the chain.

"Aww is the little lady going to cry?" the man taunted.

"Nope," Oakra replied quickly, dropping to the ground swooping her foot on the ground caused dirt to fly up so the man could not see her.

While he was trying to find her, she already knew where he was. She threw one end on the chain, wrapping it around his hand with the sword, in order to disarm the man. Then once she got the sword out of his hand, she wrapped the chain around his foot, pulling him to the ground. After that, she picked up his sword and sent it into the ground right beside his head to show that he had lost.

"I will not take his life for your entertainment, but this fight is over." Oakra declared, looking at the crowd.

With that, the guards forced her back to the living chambers of the pits and dragged the man that she had fought against.

"That has never happened before. Who won?" Nole asked, turning to Chief.

"Well, if he won, she would be dead. So just guessing, but the little lady." Chief answered.

"Oakra, you know you are supposed to kill the opponent," Nole asked, puzzled.

"I was told that, but I think it is time for a change around here," Oakra replied with a smile.

"So, she is looking to change the pits. Are you still thinking they are the only way out?" Nole asked, leaning over to Chief.

"No. Now, I know; they are our way out. After Rocky's fight is over, have them meet up with us." Chief said with a smile.

Rocky's opponent was 6'2", with a figure of a bodybuilder. He had black hair and green eyes. His choice of weapon was a battle axe, and Rocky had chosen a sword.

"Well, I get a Pipsqueak for this suit. How cute." the man taunted.

"The name is Rocky!" Rocky snapped, avoiding the axe.

Rocky slid in between the man's feet as he swung the axe into the ground. While he was fighting to get his axe free, Rocky leaped to his feet, causing the man to roll. Once he was on the ground Rocky put him in a headlock. The man struggled to get Rocky off, finally, he fell backward to try and break free. Rocky still had him in a headlock until the man passed out from lack of oxygen. The one thing Rocky didn't think of was the man passed out and fell backward on top of Rocky. Once he got out from under the man, he stood up and left the ring.

"So, you are alive, that means you won," Nole remarked as Rocky walked in.

"Yeah," Rocky replied, walking past.

"Hey, I don't know where you think you are going. Chief wants to speak with you and Oakra. Follow me." Nole responded, grabbing Rocky's arm.

"Fine, where is Oakra?" Rocky replied, looking around.

"Don't know. I have not seen her since her suite." Nole answered, as they began to walk.

"Ok, what is it that you want, Chief?" Rocky asked.

"When Oakra gets here, then I will explain," Chief answered.

"I am here." Oakra responded, walking behind them, "What is the name of this pit again?"

"It is the serpent. I am not dumb, you have been studying this building for a way out, and we want to help." Nole whispered.

"How do you know that?" Rocky question.

"Where do I start; first, you are both in the rebellion, and Oakra has been counting the guards, doors, and windows. I bet money that when she was in the ring, she was counting the security systems as well, along with the number of people in the crowd." Chief explained, "On top of that, she just asked the name of this pit."

"I know this pit. Rocky, this is where we first met." Oakra replied.

"Wait? You have been here before?" Nole asked.

"Yeah, Oakra, saved me and the Exterminator from here. Along with setting the other fighters free." Rocky explained.

"Well, that explains a lot. You broke in here before, just to save them. Do you know that if they caught you, they would have killed you, right?" Chief responded.

"Yes, but they didn't until now. Plus, this place hasn't changed a bit. So technically, they still don't have us the guard switch out every four hours. They only have three guards in the living quarters and two in the ring until it gets dark. They leave the door to the ring unlocked as well. We can use the metal rebar to climb out of the ring. Then the guards will be easy." Oakra whispered.

"Well, that is a little scary that you remembered all of that in just two weeks, but that is good," Nole replied.

"We leave tonight," Chief ordered.

"Ok, why the rush?" Rocky asked.

"Because of your stunt, you both pulled. They are putting you two in the ring tomorrow. The suit is a deathmatch. That is why we are leaving tonight." Chief explained, looking at them both nodding their heads.

That night they escaped leaving only one sign that they did. The two guards were at the entrance. Oakra made sure to leave them alive. She hit the pressure points in their necks and sides, then tied them up in front of the door. After two hours of a fast pace, the four slowed down once they came to a creek that went to Oakra's chest.

"Come on, we can find a way around it," Nole suggested, looking at it.

"Nope," Oakra replied, taking off her jacket, walking into the creek with her folded jacket being held above her head.

"Are you nuts? There is snow and ice everywhere, and you are choosing to walk through the freezing water?" Chief questioned.

"No, I am not nuts. The water makes it harder for the hounds to track us, and the snow will show footprints so the guards and troops can track us with no problem. Now, are you coming or not." Oakra explained, wading across.

"Dude, trust me. It is better to listen to her." Rocky replied following behind.

"Oh shit!!! This is freezing!!" Nole yelled.

"Keep quiet; so, we don't get caught," Oakra ordered.

It was a few hours later when the group found the rest of the rebellion.

"Blake! What in the hell happened to you?" Oakra asked, turning him around after seeing the bandages.

"Your brother challenged the guards twice and almost got run over. Name's Hestia." Hestia replied, holding her hand out.

"Nice to meet you, Hestia. Thank you for taking care of him for me." Oakra responded, shaking Hestia's hand.

"So, it looks to me as if our family has seven new members in it." Ziggy remarked, "Nice to have you all back."

"Good to be back," Oakra responded, passing the guys dry clothes.

2/10/2025

These last few weeks made me remember what it was like in the academy. It was bad for Rocky and me, but it must have been hell for Blake, judging by his back and arm. It is so nice to be back with the rest of the rebellion and my family.

Cassie

Chapter Twenty Six

Secrets Unravel

The following day, Oakra handed Blake a tablet from one of the guards at the pit.

"Here, we need as much information as possible on them. See if you can hack that." Oakra revealed, handing Blake the tablet.

"Where did you get this?" Blake asked.

"Yeah, it is a guard. So, you should have access to all of the War States files. I thought we could use it." Oakra answered.

"Well, that explains why you didn't let your jacket get wet," Nole replied, walking up behind them.

"So, what is the plan from here?" Rocky asked, looking at Oakra and Blake.

"We wait to see what Blake finds before we make another attack on them. Until then, I think we can finish turning the people against her. The government is like a tree. If the roots are not there to support it, the tree will die. The people are the roots, and the branches are the government." Oakra replied, picking up her bag.

"Wait a minute. You aren't going anywhere. They are looking for you, Rocky and Blake. If they find you, they will kill you. Someone else will go." Ziggy responded, grabbing Oakra's arm.

"That is not how things work, Ziggy. I am not sending anyone if I am not going myself. I will not be the leader who hides when things get tough. Now let go." Oakra replied, pulling her arm free.

"Fine but take someone with you then." Ziggy pleated.

"Planned on it. Ace, Nightshade, and Saturn, you guys are with me. Get your gear." Oakra remarked, picking up her bag once more.

"So, I may be new here, but does she do this a lot?" Chief asked.

"Yes, she does, and it drives me nuts!" Ziggy grunted, walking in the opposite direction.

"Still better than when we first started." Rocky chuckled.

"What does that mean?" Nole asked.

"Well, when we first started, my sister would do all the rescues and dangerous stuff by herself," Blake answered.

"You guys just let her?" Chief questioned.

"At that time, she could care less what we had to say as long as we were safe. That and everyone tried not to tick her off back then." Rocky replied.

"Why?" Nole asked.

"You saw what she did in the pits. Put a bow in her hands, then tick her off. Trust us; it won't end well." Yash jumped in.

"I see." Chief pondered.

Oakra, Ace, Nightshade, and Saturn went to the boys' hometown, where the guards had worsened since they left. When they walked in, there was a group of guards that were beating the hell out of a few civilians with batons. The four quickly took out most of the guards on the outside with long-range weapons and used hand-to-hand combat to take out the rest of them.

"Are you people, ok?" Saturn asked, helping an older man to his feet.

"Yes, thanks to you four. Wait a minute you, are officer Joe's son." the older man replied, looking at Nightshade.

"Yes, sir," Nightshade answered, turning his head away.

"He would be proud of you. I owe him my life, and now I will repay it. The people are ready to fight, but they need you guys to lead them." the old man responded, placing his hand on Nightshade's shoulder.

"You good Nightshade?" Oakra turned and asked.

"Yeah, thank you, sir," Nightshade responded.

While those four had managed to meet with the entire town, Blake found out that Odysseus was still alive. He decided to wait until Oakra, and the others got back before he said a word to anyone about it. The only problem was he could not unlock any other intel until he had better Wi-Fi.

The rebellion didn't know until now how many people were on the side. Plus, with the stunt, President Linna pulled on live TV and had turned many guards against her. Once they found out, the four told everyone to wait for them to make the first move before anyone acted that way, fewer people got hurt, and more people turned against President Linna. After they were done talking to everyone, they went back to camp.

"Oakra, I have something you all are going to want to hear and now," Blake reported as soon as he saw them walk into camp.

"What's up, Blake? This sounds serious." Oakra answered.

"It is and needs to be handled first before anything else," Blake replied, turning the tablet toward the others.

"Odysseus is still alive. We need to save him now." Blake demanded.

"Wait! Hold your horses! I might be new here, but I don't think we have to save some kid who got himself captured. Leave him until after the war is over." Chief responded, putting his hands up.

"First, let me point this out, we are not in the pits!!!! It is not every man for himself here!!!!! We are a family!! That means; we have each other's back!! Second, he is there because he wouldn't rat us out!!! Third, if it was any of us where he would do anything to save our hides!!! Fourth I am in charge here!!! Not you!! I say we are going after him first; if you have a problem with that then cry a damn river and sail a boat down it!! Don't you dare act like you know anyone here or why they are!!!" Oakra snapped, turning and meeting Chief eye to eye with rage-filled eyes.

"Ok." Chief cringed, backing away, realizing he stepped a very dangerous line.

"Rocky, Ace, Nightshade, Saturn, Yash, and Julius, you guys are with me! Blake, when we get there, kill the power. Rocky, bring the explosives! After we get Odysseus, we are going to blow the damn building to pieces." Oakra ordered, walking away.

"Dude, you had to tick her off," Yash asked, shaking his head.

"How was I supposed to know that one little suggestion would make the little lady snap like that. I didn't think someone that small could be so terrifying." Chief responded, watching her walk away.

"Yeah, she can be terrifying, but I have only seen her snap at Rocky like that. So, you should probably stay clear of her until she cools off for your safety," Yash warned and walked away.

It took them four hours to get to the building where Odysseus was being held captive. The building appeared to be a small brick house on the outside, but once Blake cut the power, they went in, but there was nothing plain about this house. It turned out this is where the War States had been keeping some of the rebellion leaders that would not turn or talk. Down the stairs, there were six cells, but only two had people in them. To their surprise, Odysseus was not the only friend that was being held captive in this prison.

"Oakra, is that you?" a familiar voice stuttered.

"Exterminator! Hang on; we are going to get you out of here." Oakra Gasped, "We thought you were killed with the rest of your group."

"Yeah, I know I heard your voices that day, but I knew if I called out to you guys, they would catch you too," Exterminator replied.

"Hang on. Back up." Oakra said, firing an arrow at the keypad lock, forcing the door to open.

"Thank you," Exterminator responded. "Odysseus, is that you?" Nightshade asked.

"About time. Hurry up before the guards come back." Odysseus answered, jumping up from his bed.

"Trust me, they aren't coming," Rocky replied.

"Ok?" Odysseus and Exterminator question.

"Someone pissed Oakra off before we came. So, unless the guards come back to life, I think we are good." Saturn answered.

"Come on, we still need to get a tablet from here and blow it up before reinforcements come," Oakra responded, walking up the stairs.

"We heard President Linna shoot her. Is she ok?" Odysseus asked.

"Umm, yeah, but I think Linna might have put a very bright target on her head after that," Yash replied.

After they grabbed the tablet, Oakra blew up the building. Then followed the others into the woods. The walk back took a little longer because Odysseus still had trouble walking due to nerve damage.

"Hey, we are back, you guys," Yash announced as he walked into camp.

"Oakra." Chief hollered, waving at her.

"Who is that?" Exterminator asked.

"Someone Oakra and I saved that seems to have a death wish," Rocky answered.

"That is an understatement." Yash jumped in.

"Blake here is another tablet. I think it should have more intel on it," Oakra revealed.

"Oakra, can I talk?" Chief asked, standing behind her.

"I have nothing to say to you. Just get out of my sight." Oakra dismissed him.

"He is pushing his luck, don't you think," Yash responded, looking at Rocky and Blake.

"Just a little bit," Blake replied.

"Oakra! Look, I am sorry! You could have easily escaped without me, and Nole but you chose to help us. I questioned you when you were going to help the kid. I understand that I don't know how things work around here and have no place to question saving someone. So, I am truly sorry for what I said." Chief apologized.

"I will let it slide this time, but next time I am just going to knock you on your ass. Am I clear?" Oakra warned.

"Yes," Chief replied and watched her walk away.

"Wow, she didn't deck you. I am shocked." Rocky chuckled.

"Maybe because he did the one thing you two fools don't do. He admitted he was wrong and apologized for it." Blake remarked, walking past.

"Hey, who's side are you on here, Blake? He is new. Why are you sticking up for him?" Yash exclaimed.

"Because he apologized, and Oakra isn't going to spend days snapping at him over it. She is normally mad at you two fools for a few days. Plus, I am on no one's side for this argument." Blake snickered, still looking at the tablet.

"I agree with the boy. All three of you guys are fools and lack any manners." Alden remarked, standing behind them.

"Oakra, guess what I just found!" Blake Exclaimed, rushing to Oakra's side.

"What is it?" Oakra asked.

"Dr. Juno's research, the formula they used to revise it and turn it into the Echidna virus, the security footage from the place before Juno torched the place, Linna's private meetings with Russia and Germany before World War three, all the phone calls she made including both of them to Officer William to shoot dad, the treaty for the War States everything!" Blake revealed everything he had found.

"Check and mate. We got our wind to turn the rest of the people." Blaze jumped in.

"Indeed, we do. Now we need just the right time to play our hand." Oakra replied, with a smile.

"You guys take a few days to rest first. I am going to see if I can find anything else. When I do, you will know." Blake responded.

"Ok as soon as you find anything else, let us know," Oakra replied.

"I will. Now please get some rest?" Blake asked.

"Fine," Oakra replied, walking away.

For the next few days, Blake kept finding more intel that could help them. They even came up with a plan on how to use it. This time they were going in armed with more people from different sides while Hestia, Alden, Agni, and Calder kept Blake safe so he could hack the emergency news broadcast to release all of the files against President Linna. This would turn the people against the guards that still choose to stand by Linna.

2/28/2025

We have grown much more in the last year. We have learned new tricks and met new people. This made us realize we were looking at how to save our country the wrong way. I thought that to save the people, we had to keep them out of this fight. Then we figured out that the only way to win this war is to expose President Linna for the devil she is. We need the people as they need us. Together we stand. It is time to finish uprooting this plant fed by greed.

Cassie

Chapter Twenty Seven

Freedom Takes Root

"Ok, Blake, you are up." Hestia signaled from a tree on the edge of the wood line.

"Hello! My name is Blake, and I am a member of the rebellion, and I have something that everyone needs to know about our dictator that claims to be the President. These are classified files that she had hidden because of her involvement in them. Some of the guards and troops that you have been dealing with for the last five years and are working for her out of fear." Blake exposed President Linna and released every file they found on live TV, "She didn't sign that treaty to help us. She signed it for power. Then they stole our freedom. Now it is our turn to take it back. Those who fear her, please don't hide. In order to win this war, we must stand together. Without each other, we will never have our freedom back. This is supposed to be the land of the free, not dictatorship. We are no monarchy, but we are a democracy. We people have feared them long enough. It is time to drive this greed and darkness out of our country."

The broadcast did just what they had hoped. Even most of the guards and troops had turned against President Linna. She now had almost no one to hide behind. Even the guards in the white house began to question her. That is when Oakra and her group made their move.

"Oakra, there are less guards here," Rocky informed her.

"I see that, but don't let your guard down because there aren't as many," Oakra replied while jumping out of a tree.

"Yash, what wing are Delilah and Alexander in?" Ace asked. "West," Yash replied, knocking out one of the guards.

"Good, Yash, Blaze, Ziggy, and Chief, you guys go get more help we have the better." Oakra ordered, "Ace, Nightshade, Odysseus, and Exterminator stay put you for are our eyes, snipe any threats. Rocky, Saturn, Julius, and Nole are with me. We are going to the oval office to take out President Linna."

With that, they split into three groups. Ace's group stayed outside and took out any reinforcements coming to President Linna's aid. Along with any escape route, including the helicopter waiting for her.

As Yash's group made their way to the west wing, Delilah and Alexander started to take out the remaining guards on their way to the other end.

"Hey, Delilah, did you two save any for us?" Yash asked.

"You are such a child. There are more coming from the east wing. Now, stop bellyaching and get ready to fight." Delilah chuckled, "Man, I have missed you, people; Linna is insane."

"You are the one who went and pulled an Oakra," Blaze responded.

"Hey, I can hear you! Next time turn off the walkie!" Oakra replied.

"Sorry, but it is true." Yash jumped in as he shot a guard behind Alexander.

"Thanks, I owe you one," Alexander responded. "Don't mention it." Yash dismissed it.

"Yash duck." Ziggy ordered as she swung her swords, removing a guard's head, "Will you two pay attention before you get killed. If you two get killed over talking in the middle of a fight, Oakra is going to resurrect you both and kill you two herself."

"Damn, now you sound like her." Yash chuckled out of fear. "West wing cleared." Blaze came across the walkie.

"We are moving in on the oval office now," Oakra responded. "Just be careful." Yash replied, "There weren't a lot of guards in the west wing, so her remaining followers are probably protecting Linna. Stay on alert."

"Yash is right there hardly anyone outside as well," Exterminator advised.

"Noted," Oakra replied, switching to her sword.

"We are coming up on the oval office, and there is still no sign of any guards. It is like they all just left." Saturn questioned.

"Hey Oakra, what is the plan when we find President Linna?" Rocky asked.

"We will capture her, and will give her a trial," Oakra answered.

"Wait! Hold it, did I hear that right? You want to leave the person who A took over the country. B killed you and Blake's father. C had you put into the academy that you hardly mention because it was hell. D has tried to kill us on numerous occasions alive. After everything, you think we should let her live?" Rocky exclaimed, looking at Oakra like she lost her mind.

"Look, I get it. I would much rather kill her too. But for us to change this country for the better, the killing must stop with Linna's capture." Oakra explained, "If we kill her without her standing a proper trial, then we are no better than her."

"So, you believe that letting her live long enough for a trial is the best thing. If so, I will back your decision." Yash replied over the walkie.

"This might backfire, but I am with you on this one," Rocky replied.

"Now, how about we go get Linna off of that throne," Saturn remarked.

"Sure thing," Nole replied, raising his gun.

When Oakra kicked open the door, no one was to be found. President Linna and her brainwashed followers had left before the rebellion had gotten there. On Linna's desktop was a paused video with a sticky note that said checkmate. Oakra hit the play button on the recording.

"So, you managed to take the white house back. Color me impressed, Cassie. I guess you and Blake are not the same kids I thought I knew. One problem is that my followers and I are long gone. We went underground the second Blake released every file. You will never find us, but when the time is right, we will be back for what is mine. Oh! Yes, Odysseus, your mother lied about who your true father was. You weren't Robert's son at all, but you are Officer William's. Consider my parting gift to you, young man. As for you, Cassie, how you are still alive puzzles me. By my count, you should have died at least three times. So, I promise you the next time we meet, I will kill you myself, but for now, checkmate. You won this, young lady." President Linna's video said.

"Oh well, I guess that answers our question about the lack of damn guards!" Rocky yelled.

"Oakra, what do we do now?" Delilah asked, walking into the room with the others.

"First, we put the next in line for the President in charge until we can do an election. Then we rebuild and hunt down Linna and her followers." Oakra answered, looking at Alexander.

"Oakra, there is no next in line; Linna killed every one of them. You are the leader of the rebellion that puts you in charge." Alexander explained.

"No, not everyone. You hold the title of Secretary Smith. That means you are the next President, not me." Oakra pointed out, "I will help rebuild, but I am not leading the entire country. You can have that job."

"Are you sure about this, Oakra?" Yash asked.

"Yes, I am. Now President Alexander, what do you want us to do?" Oakra asked with a smile.

"Been a while since we have seen you smile," Ziggy replied. "Well, we have saved our country and the people. The last thing on my to-do list, for now, is to track down Linna and drag her ass to justice." Oakra replied.

"First, you guys need to get cleaned up. Then you can go free the prisoners at the pits and fields." Alexander suggested.

"Hey, you guys, I might have some news you might like," Blake exclaimed, walking into the room with his group.

"What is that?" Oakra asked.

"I found GPS coordinates to each bunker of hers and a few secret remote prisons Linna had made before World War three," Blake answered.

"That is great. This means she can't hide from us as easily." Oakra replied.

"Before you guys do anything along those lines. Go clean up.

You will eat a decent meal and get some rest. Don't argue with me on this; you wouldn't win." Alexander ordered.

"He is right because we still have a long road ahead of us all." Oakra replied, "Together, we stand strong."

3/01/2025

I am so glad that this war has finally come to an end. There is still a long road ahead of us as a country, but we will rebuild and come back even stronger than before. I know I made the right choice placing Alexander as president. For this to work, we need to start from scratch to rebuild. I know the people will follow him. Though he will not be alone in this, the rebellion would prefer to stay out of the spotlight. We won, and now we are just here to help get things back on track. As for Linnu and her followers, they will not get away with their crimes. We will track them down and bring them to justice. There is no place for them to hide now. Like I said before, this war ends with her capture. Freedom has taken root, and the people have a new appreciation for it. I am just glad this war is finally over.

Cassie

9 7 9 8 9 8 6 0 7 1 6 1 9